SOMEWHERE SAFE

(A Piper Woods Mystery—Book 1)

Molly Black

Molly Black

Bestselling author Molly Black is author of the MAYA GRAY FBI suspense thriller series, comprising nine books (and counting); of the RYLIE WOLF FBI suspense thriller series, comprising six books; of the TAYLOR SAGE FBI suspense thriller series, comprising eight books; of the KATIE WINTER FBI suspense thriller series, comprising eleven books (and counting); of the RUBY HUNTER FBI suspense thriller series, comprising five books (and counting); of the CAITLIN DARE FBI suspense thriller series, comprising six books (and counting); of the REESE LINK mystery series, comprising six books (and counting); of the CLAIRE KING FBI suspense thriller series, comprising five books (and counting); and of the PIPER WOODS mystery series, comprising five books (and counting).

An avid reader and lifelong fan of the mystery and thriller genres, Molly loves to hear from you, so please feel free to visit www.mollyblackauthor.com to learn more and stay in touch.

ISBN: 978-1-0943-7927-2

BOOKS BY MOLLY BLACK

PIPER WOODS FBI SUSPENSE THRILLER
SOMEWHERE SAFE (Book #1)
SOMEWHERE SANE (Book #2)
SOMEWHERE WHOLE (Book #3)
SOMEWHERE FAR (Book #4)
SOMEWHERE WRONG (Book #5)

CAITLIN DARE FBI SUSPENSE THRILLER
COME GET ME (Book #1)
COME FIND ME (Book #2)
COME TAKE ME (Book #3)
COME CATCH ME (Book #4)
COME SAVE ME (Book #5)
COME STOP ME (Book #6)

MAYA GRAY MYSTERY SERIES
GIRL ONE: MURDER (Book #1)
GIRL TWO: TAKEN (Book #2)
GIRL THREE: TRAPPED (Book #3)
GIRL FOUR: LURED (Book #4)
GIRL FIVE: BOUND (Book #5)
GIRL SIX: FORSAKEN (Book #6)
GIRL SEVEN: CRAVED (Book #7)
GIRL EIGHT: HUNTED (Book #8)
GIRL NINE: GONE (Book #9)

RYLIE WOLF FBI SUSPENSE THRILLER
FOUND YOU (Book #1)
CAUGHT YOU (Book #2)
SEE YOU (Book #3)
WANT YOU (Book #4)
TAKE YOU (Book #5)
DARE YOU (Book #6)

TAYLOR SAGE FBI SUSPENSE THRILLER

DON'T LOOK (Book #1)
DON'T BREATHE (Book #2)
DON'T RUN (Book #3)
DON'T FLINCH (Book #4)
DON'T REMEMBER (Book #5)
DON'T TELL (Book #6)

KATIE WINTER FBI SUSPENSE THRILLER

SAVE ME (Book #1)
REACH ME (Book #2)
HIDE ME (Book #3)
BELIEVE ME (Book #4)
HELP ME (Book #5)
FORGET ME (Book #6)
HOLD ME (Book #7)
PROTECT ME (Book #8)
REMEMBER ME (Book #9)
CATCH ME (Book #10)
WATCH ME (Book #11)

RUBY HUNTER FBI SUSPENSE THRILLER

IF I RUN (Book #1)
IF I TELL (Book #2)
IF I LIVE (Book #3)
IF I FORGET (Book #4)
IF I RETURN (Book #5)

CAITLIN DARE FBI SUSPENSE THRILLER

COME GET ME (Book #1)
COME FIND ME (Book #2)
COME TAKE ME (Book #3)
COME CATCH ME (Book #4)
COME SAVE ME (Book #5)

REESE LINK MYSTERY

BEYOND REASON (Book #1)
BEYOND REACH (Book #2)
BEYOND REPAIR (Book #3)

BEYOND DOUBT (Book #4)
BEYOND NORMAL (Book #5)
BEYOND HOPE (Book #6)

PROLOGUE

They're not following a word I'm saying, Vanessa Johnston thought, noticing the glazed expressions of the small group of students gathered in Bakerfield University's gymnasium. They were only three or four years younger than her, and she felt a little ridiculous lecturing to them about the importance of recycling and sustainability as she gestured with the potted plant in her hand, which was thick with microgreens. To her left, one of the ecology professors, Elisha Donners, nodded at every point, smiling throughout as if by doing so she could convince the students—most of whom were taking this elective for the credits, rather than out of a genuine interest in the subject—that they weren't bored out of their gourds.

Still, this was the task her father, Elmer Johnston, had given her: touring the winter-locked state of North Dakota and speaking at various campuses, simultaneously rallying support for the so-called Green Rights bill and putting the Johnston family square in the public eye, where her father wanted it—not that there was any way to escape the public eye, not so long as he remained governor.

It didn't help that she had her own bodyguard either. Barry stood by the wall with his hands crossed in front of his groin, his black suit a dead giveaway that his only function there was to make sure nothing happened to Vanessa. She had tried to convince her dad that it was totally unnecessary—and, even worse, very uncool—to have a balding, middle-aged man follow her around, but he had insisted, reminding her that there was no harm in being careful.

He should be here doing this, not me, she thought as she pressed the clicker in her hand and turned to see a new slide projected onto the gymnasium wall, this one highlighting the massive disparity in the amount of food the earth could produce compared to how much it actually did produce.

"You can see the culprits here," she said, putting on a brave face and pretending she didn't notice how many of the students were looking anywhere but at the graph displayed on the wall. "Waste, mismanagement, political feuding—all of these things contribute to the problem. But we have the power to change it. We can make a difference by taking small steps in our own lives, like recycling, reducing our use of single-use plastics, and supporting local farmers."

As she finished speaking, Vanessa couldn't help but feel a sense of defeat. She knew that her father's Green Rights bill was little more than a publicity stunt, and that the real change needed to come from individuals and communities taking responsibility for their actions.

Just then, a group of rowdy students burst into the gymnasium, interrupting Vanessa's presentation. They were yelling and laughing, clearly not interested in listening to anything she had to say. Vanessa's heart sank as she watched the chaos unfold before her.

But then something strange happened. One of the students, a tall and muscular young man with shaggy blond hair, stepped forward and held up his hand, signaling for the others to quiet down. He looked at Vanessa with a serious expression, and then spoke in a soft but commanding voice.

"Ms. Johnston, I'm sorry for the interruption. We're just a little frustrated with all this talk about sustainability and recycling. It feels like we're not really making a difference, you know?"

Vanessa hesitated, surprised to hear such an honest question—and even more surprised by the intense gaze of those cornflower-blue eyes. She recovered quickly, however, and found herself speaking.

"Well, there are many ways to measure the impact of our actions," she began, glancing away from those unnerving eyes. "We can track our carbon footprint, monitor our waste output, and even calculate how much energy we're saving by recycling. And, of course, we can always look at the bigger picture and see how our individual actions contribute to a larger movement toward sustainability."

The guy nodded, but it was clear from his expression that this wasn't an entirely satisfactory answer. Vanessa felt a sudden urge to convince him, to show him not just how much she knew about this subject but how much it actually mattered to her. It wasn't that she wanted to impress him exactly, but something in his demeanor had struck a chord with her, and she felt a sudden desire to connect with him on a deeper level.

"Look," she said, sighing and dropping the persona she generally adopted for these events, a smiling, know-it-all version of herself that was no more organic than the water bottle Professor Donners clutched in her bracelet-clad hand, screwing and unscrewing the cap without taking a sip.

"I know that all of this can feel overwhelming," she began in a low, down-to-earth voice. "It can feel like the problems we're facing are too big for any one person to solve. But the truth is, every small action counts. Recycling just one plastic bottle might not feel like a big deal at the moment, but over time, those actions add up. And if we all start taking responsibility for our own impact on the environment, I promise you, we can create real change."

The young man looked at her for a long moment, and Vanessa felt the weight of his gaze like a physical thing. She could see the skepticism in his eyes, but there was something else there, too—something that made her heart race a little faster.

He took a breath to speak, but before he could get any words out, Professor Donners cleared her throat loudly. "I'm afraid that's all the time we have for now," she said. "If you have any questions, there are brochures available in the back of the room. Thank you, Ms. Johnston, for your time and for sharing your knowledge with us."

Vanessa felt a pang of disappointment as the students began to file out of the gymnasium, their chatter filling the air as they made their way toward their next classes. She searched for the blue-eyed young man, hoping he would stick around, but she was distracted by the sound of Barry's voice.

"You did good, kid," he said in that monotone voice of his, his half-lidded eyes making him look perpetually drunk. He glanced at his watch. "We're supposed to be over in Heatherton by ten, so we should shake a leg."

Vanessa nodded, depressed at the idea of giving yet another talk, passing out yet another handful of pins, as if by doing so they could secure votes for her father in the next election. She was twenty-two, for goodness' sake, a grown woman. So why didn't she have her own life? She felt like an extension of her father, a puppet on a string, doing his bidding and living *his* dream rather than her own. It was about time she carved out her own identity, pursued her own passions.

One of the professors, a short redhead with curled bangs, moseyed over to Barry, giving him a coy glance.

"So you work for the governor, huh?" she asked, her words glowing with praise as if they were talking about winning a gold medal in the Olympics.

"That's right," Barry said, looking surprised by the sudden attention. He colored a little, and Vanessa turned away, rolling her eyes.

Even Barry has someone to talk to. But who do I have?

Just then she caught sight of the blue-eyed guy stepping into the hallway that ran along the gymnasium. As he did so, he paused to look back, his gaze both curious and…what was it…inviting?

"—so exciting," the redhead was saying, a thrill in her voice. "You must have so many stories to tell."

Barry played it off with an air of insincere modesty. "Oh, it's not that big of a deal. Just my way of serving my country."

"I'll be right back," Vanessa said, pushing past him and heading toward the door through which the young man had disappeared.

"Hold up," Barry said, frowning as he turned toward her. "Where are you going?"

She spun around, spreading her arms wide. "To the bathroom. Is that okay, or do you need to follow me in there, too?"

Barry gave an embarrassed chuckle and glanced at the redhead. "She's a character, this one," he said, gesturing at Vanessa. "Don't be gone long, okay?"

"I'll meet you at the car," she said. Then she hurried off before he could change his mind. Ordinarily he would have stuck to her like a flea to a dog, but he was clearly too distracted to take his duties as literally as he usually did, which was just fine with Vanessa.

Finally, some freedom, she thought as she moved through the doorway and continued down the hallway, her eyes quickly scanning the classroom doors for any sign of the blue-eyed guy. She wasn't entirely sure what she intended to do—she hardly even knew a thing about him, after all—but she felt a desperate need for adventure, a sense that not everything in the world could be scheduled and broken down into a neat formula. She wanted excitement, the unknown, a sense of mystery and even perhaps danger.

Her life as a governor's daughter was far too predictable, far too safe. It was time to set the script aside for once and see what happened.

Her heartbeat accelerated as she embraced this new perspective if only for a little while. As she continued down the hallway, however, a sense of unease crept up on her. She saw no sign of the guy, and she wasn't about to poke her head into the classrooms and see if he was in there.

Where did he go? she thought, pausing and looking around. *Did I misread him?*

She turned around, half expecting to see Barry striding toward her, but to her surprise he was nowhere to be seen. For once, he hadn't followed her, and she wasn't sure whether she was pleased or distressed by this.

Then she heard a footstep behind her, and she spun around, surprised.

"Sorry, didn't mean to startle you," the young man said, pawing his hair away from his eyes. Up close, he was even better-looking than Vanessa had noticed before. She felt a thrill of excitement run through her.

"Hey," she said, clearing her throat and trying to think what to say. "I didn't catch your name earlier."

He shrugged, his eyes flickering with amusement. "I didn't give it."

Vanessa smiled, feeling a sudden impulse to tease him. "Well, that's not very fair, is it? You know my name, after all."

He chuckled, stuffing his hands into his pockets. "Alright, you got me there. My name's Owen."

"Nice to meet you, Owen," Vanessa said, holding out her hand. He took it, his grip firm and warm. Vanessa felt a jolt of electricity shoot through her at the contact, and she wondered why she felt so drawn to him. Was it the thrill of danger, the excitement of the unknown, or was there something more? She couldn't quite put her finger on it.

"What are you still doing here?" Owen asked. "I thought you'd be out of here like a cat with its tail on fire as soon as you were done. You looked miserable up there."

Vanessa's face crumpled with disappointment. "Was it that bad?"

He gave another of his devil-may-care shrugs. "It wasn't bad, per se. It's just that you seemed like you were doing it more for your father's sake than your own. Seemed like your mind was somewhere else, but your mouth kept moving."

Vanessa sighed. To her surprise, she found herself confiding in this stranger. Maybe she felt safe with him because she'd probably never see him again, or because he didn't seem to care one way or the other whether everything she said lined up with her father's views.

"I'm used to it, honestly," she said with a long sigh. "My father's a politician, and I'm always being sent around to events like this."

Owen raised his eyebrows ironically. "Sounds like a real glamorous life."

Vanessa rolled her eyes. "Oh, it's glamorous, all right. If you're into being scrutinized every moment of the day and always having to watch what you say and do."

"So screw it."

For a moment, Vanessa could only stare at him, surprised by this blunt response. "What?" she asked.

"I said, screw it. Screw your father's expectations, screw what you're supposed to do. What do you really want to do?"

Vanessa felt a twinge of excitement at the question. It was something she had been asking herself for a long time, but had never quite been able to put into words. Now, standing in front of this handsome stranger with his devil-may-care attitude, she felt like she could be honest with him.

"I'm not sure," she admitted. "I've always felt like I'm living someone else's life: my father's life, my mother's life, the life of a politician's daughter. I want something more. Something real."

Owen nodded, a small smile playing at the corners of his lips. "Well, that's a start. So, what do you like to do? What makes you happy?"

Vanessa was thinking about this when she began to get the odd feeling she was being watched. She turned toward the window just as a shape moved past, as if someone had been standing outside, watching her. All she could see now, however, was a crust of snow leading back toward the school's soccer field.

It was probably just a bird darting by, she told herself. *Nothing more.*

She felt a sudden urge to get away, to leave this place and everything that was weighing her down. And then, without warning, something inside her snapped and she knew what she needed to do.

"Let's get out of here," she said, turning to Owen with a determined look on her face.

He raised his eyebrows, surprised by her sudden change in attitude. "What do you mean?"

"I mean, let's leave this place. Let's go somewhere and do something different, something real. I'm tired of living in a bubble, of pretending to be someone I'm not. I want to experience life, to really live it."

Owen's eyes sparkled with excitement, as if he'd just been looking for an excuse to play hooky. "I'm in." He pulled a set of car keys from his pocket. "I've got wheels, too."

That was all Vanessa needed to hear. Without another word, she took Owen's hand and began to lead him toward the exit. She felt a sense of exhilaration wash over her, a feeling that she was finally taking control of her own life. She didn't know where they were going or what they were going to do, but she didn't care. A sense of familial responsibility would return to her eventually, she knew, but for now she was more than willing to ride this high of independence.

As she pushed open the door and stepped into the gray light of an overcast winter morning, however, Owen's hand slipped from hers.

"Left my backpack inside," he said. "I'll be just a minute."

Vanessa nodded, trying not to be disappointed. She sensed that time was of the essence—that if she waited too long, if she gave the voice of inner logic enough chances to dissuade her, it would convince her she needed to find Barry and stick to the schedule she'd agreed on with her father. What was she planning to do with Owen, anyway? They were complete strangers, knowing little of each other beyond first names.

Everyone has to grow up eventually, she heard her father say, repeating a refrain he had used a thousand times before. But she was not ready to grow up, not ready to embrace all the tedious responsibilities that made her parents' lives so colorless: carefully planned dinners with important guests, endless meetings and charity events, photo ops with her father's constituents, and the constant pressure to maintain an image of perfection.

No, she wanted something different, something unscripted and spontaneous. She deserved that much.

"Come on," she muttered, pacing across the sidewalk running along the perimeter of the brick building. Then she heard a muffled curse, followed by the clatter of metal, and she turned to see a bearded man kneeling beside a van on the street, a steel tool on the asphalt beside him.

A tire iron, she thought, but she knew this was not quite right, remembered that her father had called it something else—a wrench of some kind. It seemed important somehow, as if her self-image depended upon this mental exercise.

The bearded man caught Vanessa looking. He sighed and shook his head, smiling wryly. "Damn lug nut won't turn," he said.

Lug wrench. Yes, that's what it's called.

"You have to jump on it," she said, maintaining a wary distance. This wariness was not so much a feature of her personality as it was a product of her father's many cautions. According to Elmer Johnston, the world was full of dangerous people just looking for an opportunity to use someone else's vulnerability to their advantage—which was why his daughter had to walk around with a bodyguard in tow.

With a defeated shrug, as if he already knew any such attempt would end in failure, the bearded man fit the wrench back on the nut and placed one foot on it. As he placed his weight on it, however, his foot slipped and he landed hard on his knee, grimacing.

The man's clumsiness won out over Vanessa's borrowed wariness. She couldn't bear to watch his pathetic attempts any longer—it felt cruel, like ignoring a child's attempts at grasping a toy just out of reach.

Striding forward, compelled by an automatic desire to help, she waved a hand at him to stop. "Here, let me help," she said. "My dad showed me how."

As she neared the van—an ancient-looking thing, yellow on the bottom and white on the top, the kind of vehicle her parents might have used on a camping trip when they were teenagers—she glanced at the tire in question. She could see nothing wrong with it—it appeared to be inflated to the appropriate size, and there were no signs of damage to suggest the tire's durability had been compromised. She was so focused on demonstrating how to remove the lug nuts, however, that she hardly noticed this.

The bearded man slipped the lug wrench back on the nut, then stepped back, planting his hands on his hips as he waited for her to demonstrate.

Vanessa took a deep breath and put her foot on the wrench. She pushed down with all her might, but the wrench did not move—the nut was fixed tight. Sensing she was probably dealing with rust, she lifted her left foot off the ground and used all her weight to bounce on the lug nut.

Suddenly it came free, and the wrench dropped to the ground like a seesaw.

She staggered, both embarrassed and exultant, and turned to see the bearded man's reaction. She was surprised to discover the door of the van was standing open. Inside, she could see a tarp spread across the seat and floor, and on this tarp rested a coil of rope and a roll of duct tape.

Unease stirred inside Vanessa, as if she had swallowed a snake. She took a quick step back, her unease rapidly graduating to panic. It was too late, however—the baseball bat in the man's hand told her so.

"Sorry, darling," he said.

And then he swung.

CHAPTER ONE

Piper Woods stopped abruptly as she came across the boot prints in the snow, her heart giving a sharp jolt inside her chest. The prints were heading straight toward her cabin.

Who in the world could this be? she thought with a twinge of unease, feeling as if she had just come home to find a stranger's jacket hanging beside the door.

She lived off the grid in Alaska's rugged Brooks Range, a six-hundred-mile stretch of mountains that curved east to west across the state's northern half. It was an inhospitable place, wild and treacherous, home to polar bears, wolverines, and wolves. Even more deadly than its predators, however, was its cold. The temperature routinely dropped to negative fifty degrees Fahrenheit in the winter, with snow coming eight to nine months of the year.

In short, it was not the sort of place people happened upon by accident. And they certainly didn't come across Piper's remote cabin simply by getting lost.

So how'd they get here? And what do they want?

A thrill of uncertainty ran through her. She straightened, listening carefully to the rustling of the trees, smelling the damp lichen and the scent of pine needles. Without realizing she was doing it, she was on the hunt again, using the fine-honed instincts her father, "Lucky" Luke, had taught her during their many years living in the wilderness together. He'd been a tracker for the Alaskan state police, a brilliant—if sometimes paranoid—survivalist whose lifestyle had embodied the idea of "roughing it," and he and Piper had spent many days stalking game together, learning to read the signs of the wilderness and to live off the land.

It was the disappearance of Piper's mother, Ila, that had caused Piper and her father to set out on their own, leaving their family homestead just north of Anchorage. Ila had gone on a trip to visit family in a village about twenty miles away, a journey she took once a year, and this time Luke and Piper had stayed behind to take care of the homestead. Ila, however, never reached her family, nor was her body ever discovered.

Supposing his family must've been targeted, Luke took Piper away from the homestead, heading deeper into the wilderness and avoiding contact with civilization as much as possible. This motile lifestyle had engendered in Piper a distrust and lack of familiarity with modern technology, but it had also taught her to survive in the wild.

And, among other things, to track game.

Piper tapped into those skills now as she followed the tracks up the hill, the snow crunching softly beneath her snowshoes. She unslung her rifle, a Remington 700, and held it low in both hands as she moved, her eyes carefully scanning the trees. She knew this forest intimately, had crossed and recrossed it countless times, and she searched for anything that did not belong here, her mind still puzzling over the mystery of who would have visited her.

As she came over the brow of the hill and saw her cabin standing in a small clearing ahead of her, a thick plume of smoke billowing from the chimney, she stopped in her tracks. At first she thought she might be looking at a bear—it was not uncommon for her to find a grizzly poking around her camp, searching for a way into the small box she called home, even though she had built this cabin with her father and knew it could withstand the attack of even the most persistent bear.

Upon further inspection, however, she realized she was not looking at a bear but at a large man clad in a parka and snow pants, his hands covered with thick gloves, his face hidden behind a ski mask. He looked vaguely familiar to Piper, but she could not be sure, not from this distance.

She stayed where she was and studied the man for a few moments, watching him stomp his feet and clap his hands together to keep them warm, occasionally knocking on the door. He said something, and at first Piper couldn't catch the word. Then he repeated it, and the wind drew the sound to her ears.

He was calling her name.

Even more puzzled than before, Piper stepped out of hiding and approached, still keeping the rifle low but ready to raise it at a moment's notice. As the man returned to his pacing, he glanced up and noticed her.

"Damn, Pip. You just about scared the shit out of me."

She knew that voice—besides, there was nobody else in the world who called her by that nickname. It was her former FBI partner, Lawrence Wade.

"Wade?" she asked, unable to hide her surprise. "What are you doing here?"

He chuckled dryly. "Oh, just thinking of buying real estate in the area. Thought I'd talk to you, see what you think of the neighbors."

For a few heartbeats, she just stared at him in confused silence. She'd forgotten how sarcastic he could be.

"How'd you find me?" she asked.

"Do we really need to have this conversation out here? I'm freezing my ass off."

Piper had also forgotten how much Wade disliked the cold. She hurried forward and unlocked the door. They stepped inside and she quickly closed the door behind them, blocking out the biting Alaska wind.

"So," Wade said, looking around the small, one-room cabin, "this is your place, huh?" It was clear from the tone of his voice that he was unimpressed. Not that Piper was surprised—he was a city boy, through and through, born and raised on the mean streets of Detroit. He wouldn't be caught dead staying somewhere without internet access and a flat-screen TV, never mind electricity and running water.

Hanging her rifle on a wall peg, Piper stripped off her gloves and hung them above the stove. Then she opened the stove's door, broke up the embers with a poker, and began filling the stove's belly with wood again.

"You're the last person in the world I'd expect to see out here," she said.

He grunted. "With good reason. How do you hack it?"

She gestured vaguely toward the door. "I've got a well for water, solar panels for the lights, enough caribou meat saved up to last me the winter even if I stopped hunting today. If I need any extra supplies, I head over to Eagle Point."

Wade pulled off his gloves, followed by his mask. It was Lawrence Wade, alright. His jaw was a little rounder, his facial hair a little thicker, but otherwise he was the same as she remembered.

Wade held his large hands over the stove, absorbing the heat. "What happens when you get snowed in?"

"I tunnel out," Piper said with a shrug. "I've survived plenty of harsh winters before. I know how to make it through. My mother was half-Inuit, remember."

Wade shook his head, looking around the cabin with a mixture of disbelief and distaste. "Still, it's gotta be lonely as hell. Then again, you always did like flying solo."

It was strange, hearing his voice again. Once upon a time, she and Wade had been close. They'd never dated, but at times such a thing had seemed almost inevitable, as if they were two asteroids set on a collision course with one another. But a full year had passed since she'd left the Bureau. How much had changed since then?

Wade cleared his throat and began rummaging in one of his parka's massive pockets. "Listen, I brought you something." He held out his hand, revealing a pile of wrapped candies, each a different color than the rest.

"Saltwater taffy," Piper said, smiling and shaking her head in surprise. "My favorite. You remembered."

Wade grinned, looking pleased with himself. "Of course I remembered. I may not be a wilderness expert like you, but I know a thing or two about candy preferences."

Piper took the taffy from him and unwrapped a piece, popping it into her mouth. The sweet and salty taste flooded her senses and she closed her eyes, savoring it. It had been a long time since she'd had a treat like this.

"Thanks," she said, opening her eyes again and giving him a small smile. "It's good to see you again, Wade."

"It's good to see you too, Pip." He set the pile of candy on a shelf. Then he leaned back against the wall, his eyes trailing over her as if taking in her appearance for the first time. "You look good. Tougher than ever."

"I *am* tougher than ever," she said, taking another piece of taffy from the pile. "I have to be, out here on my own."

"Still, ain't no crime to have a cell phone. I could've called instead of dragging my sorry ass halfway across Siberia."

The tension thickened, and Piper sensed he wasn't entirely being facetious. Needing to give herself something to do, she began preparing two mugs of tea. It was a bitter concoction, caffeine-free and made from roots she'd harvested, good for digestion and, more importantly, warming to the body.

Wade let out a long sigh. "Well, one way or the other, I'm here now. The short of it is, Pip, the Bureau wants you back."

She glanced sharply at him, ready to protest, but he cut her off with an upraised hand.

"Hold your horses. I'm not talking about a full-time job, not like it used to be. One case, that's all. Truth is, you're the best option we have."

"I find that hard to believe. I've been out of the Bureau for the past year. Are you telling me in all that time, you haven't found anyone to replace me?"

He stared at the stove, which gave off an intermittent ticking as the metal expanded. "Who can do what you do?" He shook his head. "Nobody."

Piper fell silent, not sure what to make of this. As much as she appreciated the compliment, she didn't like having to tell Wade he had wasted his time by coming all the way out here.

She poured the tea—the kettle had been sitting on the stove when they arrived, lending some moisture to the dry air—and then passed one of the mugs to Wade. He took one sniff and recoiled as if there were a spider crouching in the bottom of the mug.

"Just try it," she said. "You'll feel better."

Grimacing, he sipped the steaming tea. He made a queasy face and set the mug aside.

"There's a girl missing, Vanessa Johnston," he began, cutting right to the chase. "Daughter of South Dakota's state governor, Elmer Johnston. She was at a university campus, giving a talk on ways to help the environment—raising support for a bill her father's been pushing—when she vanished out of thin air. Her bodyguard, Barry Greenwood, let her out of his sight for just a few minutes. Apparently that was enough."

Piper sipped her tea and frowned, already knowing where this was going. "Let me guess: The Bureau suspects foul play."

Wade nodded, his face serious. "We think she was kidnapped. A few students saw a yellow vehicle driving away from the school—an RV, by the sound of it."

"Do you think it's politically motivated? A way to get at her father—blackmail, maybe?"

Wade picked up his mug and studied it dubiously, as if uncertain whether to try the bitter brew again. "I'm guessing you don't have any coffee?"

"Fresh out."

He set the mug down again. "It's too early to say for sure. All we know right now is that we've got a high-profile kidnapping on our hands. The governor's office is putting pressure on us to find her, and fast."

"Which is why you came to me," Piper said.

"Which is why I came to you."

"Because you think I can track her down."

"Can't you?"

She sighed, staring thoughtfully at the floor. "I don't know, Wade. There's a reason I left the Bureau in the first place."

"Because you needed a break," he said. "And you've had it."

That was not entirely true, and Wade knew it. Piper had left the Bureau because her last case, a slew of killings perpetrated by a sociopath named Byron Gray, had ended in utter failure. Piper had failed to capture Gray or prevent him from taking the life of his last victim, Fiona Taylor, and the memory of that investigation was like a stain on Piper's mind. She carried the guilt with her every day like a pile of stones in her backpack.

"Come on, Pip," Wade pressed. "This is what you were born to do. You were meant to be out there, hunting down the bad guys. It's in your blood."

Piper rubbed her hands slowly together, staring at the light flickering around the vents on the door of the stove. She rose, adjusted the damper on the stovepipe to reduce the hot air's escape, and then sat down again.

"I don't know if I'm ready to go back to that," she said in a soft, thoughtful voice. "Hunting killers, tracking down missing people…" She glanced up, meeting Wade's eyes. "It takes a toll on you. Mentally, emotionally. It's not something you can just turn on and off like a switch."

Wade gestured at the numerous pelts hanging from the wall. "Look around you, Pip! This is what you do—you track, you hunt. You're still doing it every day."

She shook her head. "That's not the same. I'm tracking animals, not people. Animals don't have the same motives, the same intelligence, the same…deviousness."

Wade let out a deep sigh. He scrubbed at his face, looking suddenly tired, and Piper wondered if he was realizing that this entire trip had been a waste.

"Listen," he said. "I wouldn't ask if I didn't think this was life-or-death. But I've seen plenty of kidnappings like this, and I've gotta tell you, if there ain't a ransom note within the first twenty-four hours—and there hasn't been one—they don't usually end well."

He paused, giving Piper time to speak. She remained silent, mulling over his words.

She couldn't deny that there was a part of her that missed the thrill of the chase, the satisfaction of bringing a killer to justice. But she also couldn't forget the toll it had taken on her: the nightmares, the anxiety attacks, the fear that she would see Byron Gray's face again—peering at her in the reflection of a shop window, staring at her in a restroom mirror, leering at her from the darkness of an alley.

Wade reached into his pocket and pulled out a phone with a thick antenna. “This is a satellite phone,” he said, setting it on the shelf. “I’ll leave it here in case you change your mind. Think about it, but don’t take too long—time isn’t on our side. Or on Vanessa’s, for that matter.”

Piper pressed her lips together sympathetically as she looked up at her former partner. She sensed there was something she was supposed to say or do, some way to express that it had been good to see him and she wished him well, but the words sounded artificial to her ears, so she remained silent. The tension thickened, and she thought of all the stakeouts they had gone on together, all the meals and rambling conversations to while away the time. It all seemed like a half-remembered dream now.

“It was good seeing you,” Wade said, hesitating a moment longer. Then he opened the door, stepped out into the bitter cold of the Alaska afternoon, and disappeared, leaving Piper to stare into her bitter tea and ponder his words.

CHAPTER TWO

The satellite phone was like a living presence beside Piper, and she found her gaze continually cutting to it as she moved about the cabin, sweeping the floor and scrubbing her pot for dinner and keeping herself busy with other daily chores.

She couldn't stop thinking about Wade's request, about the missing girl and the pressure he was under to find her. The thought of diving back into the world of crime and investigation made her stomach churn, but at the same time, she couldn't deny how good it felt to be needed.

What if she really was the only one who could help? What if she could actually save Vanessa Johnston's life?

Don't forget what happened the last time you tried to save someone, she thought. Her failure to save Fiona was the very reason she had left the Bureau. What if it happened again? What if she tried to save Vanessa, only to fail? How would she live with herself?

Tormented by these thoughts, she slipped her jacket, gloves, and hat back on, plucked the rifle off the wall, and set out to gather more firewood. She grabbed her sled from the side of the cabin and dragged it along a familiar trail, her eyes searching for deadwood while her mind wandered to memories of her father.

Luke Woods had been the very definition of a loner, a man more at peace in the wilderness than in civilization. Working as a tracker for the Alaska state police had offered him the opportunity to spend long stretches of time in the backcountry, sometimes disappearing for weeks as he hunted down fugitives or searched for missing hikers. He had instilled in Piper a deep respect for the land, for the animals that called it home, and for the survival skills necessary to live in such a harsh environment. Sometimes she felt like her cabin, with its pelts and furs and hunting trophies, was a tribute to his memory.

He had been an inveterate loner, yes…but despite that, he'd never turned down someone in need. Piper remembered one summer when a group of hikers had gotten lost in the mountains. Her father had spent days searching for them without a second thought, and when he finally found them, he had stayed with them until they were rescued. His selflessness had always been an inspiration to her.

She wondered what he would do in her situation. Would he turn his back on a girl in need, or would he rise to the challenge and do whatever it took to save her?

He had his limits, too, she thought, snapping branches off a fallen tree. *He couldn't save Mom, after all.*

When Ila disappeared, Luke spent months searching for her, barely eating or sleeping as he continually traced and retraced the trail his wife had hiked, searching for some clue as to what had happened to her but finding nothing. The police thought she had been attacked by a wild animal, a theory that seemed to Piper to be the most likely scenario, but Luke was adamant there had been foul play. He would not explain his reasoning to Piper, however—he insisted it was not her burden to carry, as if she wasn't already sharing the burden by witnessing the toll it took on him.

Eventually Luke left his job, and shortly thereafter he abandoned the homestead, convinced someone would be coming after Piper.

He could have saved more lives by returning to his work, but he didn't.

Instead of that, Luke had taken Piper all across the state, moving from one camp to another, always convinced they were being watched. Piper couldn't help wondering if this constant anxiety had contributed to his fatal heart attack several years earlier.

Troubled by these memories, she tossed a few more sticks on the sled and then began dragging it back toward the cabin. The sun was already sinking, the shadows growing long across the forest, and soon the temperature would plunge. All she wanted to do was to eat some jerky, crawl into bed, and get some sleep.

She left the sled outside, not bothering to unload it yet. She would do so tomorrow. Entering the cabin, she steadfastly ignored the satellite phone as she ate her jerky and stoked the fire. Then she undressed, crawled into bed, and closed her eyes.

I'm done with that life, she thought, turning her face toward the wall.

* * *

She dreamed she was in a large tunnel, water coursing past her feet. It was a storm drain, and the heavy rains above were causing torrents of water to splash into the tunnel, foaming and crashing like waves at sea.

A scream echoed down the tunnel. *Fiona!* she thought, hurrying forward, drawing her sidearm as she went. She had to stop Gray before it was too late.

As she followed a curve in the tunnel, she saw a light dancing ahead of her. Dimly she could make out two figures, Gray dragging Fiona along by the hair while she fought to escape him.

"Stop!" Piper shouted, racing forward. No matter how fast she ran, however, she didn't seem able to close the distance. The water rose until it was at the height of her waist, slowing her.

The tunnel branched, and Piper saw Gray drag Fiona to the right. She tried to follow, but just then a massive surge of water hit her from behind, carrying her down the left tunnel. She tried to stop herself, tried to fight against the current, but it was impossible. Turning around, she caught one final glimpse of Fiona's face, her tearful eyes begging Piper to do something, and then Piper was gone, coughed out into a dark and numbing sea.

She woke up gasping for breath, her heart pounding. It took a few moments for her to remember where she was.

"It's okay," she told herself aloud. "You're safe."

Even so, she found herself reaching for her rifle, comforted by the feel of it in her hands.

"It was just a dream," she said into the silence of the room. "Nothing but a dream." Even though these words were true, they didn't *feel* true. The dream might have been imaginary, but the feelings it represented—and the facts of what had happened during that case—were not.

She sat on the edge of the bed, waiting for her racing heart to calm down. Her eyes shifted to the satellite phone.

You can't save Fiona, she thought. *But maybe, just maybe, you can save Vanessa.*

All at once, she came to a decision. She wasn't going to keep running, as her father had done. She was tired of the nightmares, the anxiety attacks, the memories that wouldn't go away.

Slipping out of bed, she walked over to the phone and picked it up. She dialed Wade's number with shaking fingers.

"Hello?" he answered, sounding groggy. And no wonder—it was past midnight.

"Wade, it's Piper," she said, her voice barely above a whisper.

"Pip. Is everything okay?"

She hesitated, not sure how to answer the question. Her heart was still racing, and when she closed her eyes, she could still hear Fiona's scream, still see her pleading face.

"I'll help you find Vanessa," she said. "But that's all—just this one time."

There was a long pause on the other end of the line before Wade finally spoke.

"Are you sure about this, Pip? Don't do this just for me."

"I'm not. I'm doing it for her." *And for me,* she added mentally. *Because I don't want to keep running.*

There was another pause. When Wade spoke again, there was a note of relief in his voice. "Okay. I'll send a helicopter in the morning, then we can catch a flight to North Dakota. I'm really glad you changed your mind, Pip."

She bit her lip and said nothing, still not entirely certain whether she was making the right choice. If this backfired and she failed again—but no, she couldn't think that way.

"Get some sleep, Pip," Wade said. "You'll need it."

"You, too, Wade."

The call ended, and Piper stared down at the phone in her hand, feeling a mixture of excitement and dread. She had just agreed to return to the life she had left behind, to face the danger and the darkness once again, even if it was only for this one case.

She thought of her father, and the dark path he had gone down after Ila's appearance, becoming consumed with paranoia and cutting himself off entirely from the outside world. As much as Piper wanted to avoid her father's mistakes, she knew there was a good chance something similar might happen to her if she failed again.

If she tried to save Vanessa and came up short, as she had with Fiona, she just might cut herself off from the rest of the world forever—

And hide herself so far away that not even a man as determined as Wade would be able to find her again.

CHAPTER THREE

Somewhere down there, Piper thought, *my parents' bones are buried.*

It felt surreal, staring out the window of the airplane as the Alaska countryside rolled beneath them, a snowy wilderness of rugged mountains and majestic lakes. It had felt like home to her all her life, and for the past year she had believed she might never leave it again.

Yet here she was, on a plane to South Dakota with her former partner beside her, ready to get back into the work she had so abruptly left. How had things changed so quickly?

"Not second-guessing your decision, are you?" Wade asked, popping a pretzel into his mouth as he watched her.

"No," she said, frowning as she gathered her thoughts. "Just can't believe I'm doing this."

He grinned at her. "Just like old times, eh, partner?"

"That's what I'm afraid of." She raised her eyebrows knowingly at him to signal that she was joking.

He nudged her playfully. "Oh, come on. We always made a good team."

"You mean *I* made a good team and you just followed along," she teased.

Wade chuckled. "Hey, I was the muscle to your brains."

They both laughed, and Piper felt her nerves begin to ease. Maybe this wouldn't be so awkward after all. Maybe she could slip back into her old role without too much trouble.

She studied her partner, her smile fading. "Seriously, though, how have you been?" She was wondering, among other things, whether he was married now, but she wasn't about to come out and ask such a blunt question. He wasn't wearing a ring, but that didn't necessarily mean anything. She knew some agents who removed their rings whenever they were on the job, a subtle way of preventing the criminals they dealt with from using such information against them.

"I've been good," Wade replied. "Just trying to keep up with the work. You know how it is."

Piper nodded, relieved that he didn't seem to notice her awkwardness. "Yeah, I do."

The conversation lagged for a moment, and Piper gazed out the window again. She couldn't help but feel a sense of nostalgia as she studied the snow-covered landscape, a sense of wordless longing. She didn't know if she was longing for the wilderness she had just left or for the life she'd had a year ago, back before she left the Bureau.

"What about you?" Wade asked, breaking the silence. "How have you been? Is the hermit's life everything you dreamed?"

Piper hesitated, not sure how much to reveal. Wade knew her reasons for leaving the Bureau—they'd had more than one heated exchange as he tried to convince her to stay—but they hadn't maintained any contact since then, not least of all because Piper had chosen not to keep a cell phone, computer, or other way to access the outside world. She wasn't sure if she was ready to open up to him completely, at least not just yet.

"I've been…adjusting," she said finally, avoiding his eyes. "Figuring out what life looks like for me now."

Wade nodded, his sharp eyes studying her. How much could he see?

She cleared her throat, uncomfortable beneath this scrutiny. "So," she said, "do you have a case file or something?"

In answer, Wade bent and unzipped the duffel bag at his feet, pulling out a manila folder. It was thin, with only a few pages inside, a clear indication of how little information they had to go on.

He passed it over to Piper, who took it with a sense of unease. Up to this point, all she'd done was have a conversation with Wade and hop onto a plane. As soon as she started reading this file, however, her real work would begin, and there would be no going back.

Taking a breath to brace herself, she opened the file and stared at a picture of Vanessa Johnston clipped to the page. She appeared to be in her early twenties, perhaps the same age as Fiona Taylor. Also like Fiona, her hair was long, blonde, and straight, and she had a bright smile, both cheerful and innocent, as if looking toward a future from which no evil could possibly arise.

"You alright?" Wade asked.

"Yeah." She hesitated, swallowing. "It's just…she looks a lot like Fiona."

Wade nodded, his dark eyes studying her carefully.

"Can I get you something to drink?" a flight attendant asked, pausing with a hand on the back of Wade's seat.

"No, thanks," he answered without looking away from Piper's face. After the attendant had moved on, he said, "You're not trapped back there, you know. In the past. It's a new day."

She nodded, appreciating his attempt to encourage her. The words did not feel true, however. She had failed to rescue Fiona, and now she was being called back into the world of danger and darkness to try to save another young woman. It was hard not to feel trapped by her past failures, even if she knew she had to move forward.

Returning her attention to the file, Piper flipped through the pages, reading the scant details of the investigation so far. It wasn't much to go on, but she was used to working with less.

As she read, Piper felt a familiar excitement bubbling up inside her. This was what she had been trained for, what she had always been good at: finding people, piecing together clues, and bringing criminals to justice. It was what had driven her for years—up until her encounter with Gray, that was.

"The only lead we have so far," Wade said, "is that yellow RV seen leaving the school at the time of Vanessa's disappearance. We haven't been able to track the vehicle down yet, though."

"Any description of the driver?" Piper asked.

"A big-looking, bearded man."

Piper arched an eyebrow. "Sounds like you."

Wade reached up to stroke his goatee, which was perhaps a quarter inch long. "Nah, his is longer—thicker, too. Ear to ear, by the sound of it."

"It looks good, by the way," Piper found herself saying. "The goatee. Makes you seem a bit more…rugged."

He grunted. "If I listen to you, you'll have me looking like Jeremiah Johnson in no time."

She laughed at that, and he grinned back at her. For a moment, it felt just like old times. Then the plane hit turbulence, breaking the moment, and Piper grew serious again.

"Where are you thinking we should start?" she asked.

Wade shifted in his seat and leaned his head back. "I'll take you to headquarters and introduce you. We've got the whole circus for this one: police, U.S. marshals, a few other Bureau agents—and us, of course."

"Sounds busy," Piper said, feeling a bit uncomfortable at the thought of working with such a large task force. She preferred to go solo most of the time, as her father had done. Wade was the only other person she had ever felt comfortable sharing her thoughts and theories with, and he was probably the only person in the world who could have convinced her to leave her Alaska cabin. She did not relish the prospect of having so many cooks in the kitchen, especially not when multiple agencies were involved. It was too easy for interdepartmental conflict to get in the way of actual investigative work.

"That's how Governor Johnston wants it," Wade said, closing his eyes. "All hands on deck. And he's got a lot of pull." He took a deep breath and let it out slowly. "You should get some rest, Pip. I have a feeling we may not get many chances later on."

Piper nodded, even though Wade couldn't see her, and turned toward the window. The truth was, she wouldn't have been able to sleep even if she had wanted to. Already her mind was turning with the details of the case, thinking about that yellow RV and its bearded driver.

Besides, sleep wasn't always the safe haven for her that it was for Wade. Sleep was a place for her worst fears to surface.

As she stared at the islands of cloud below her, she kept picturing Vanessa's face without meaning to, unsettled by how similar the girl looked to Fiona.

Would it be different this time? Would she succeed with Vanessa where she had failed with Fiona?

And would she be able to live with herself if she failed yet again?

* * *

Well, this is familiar, Piper thought, watching as Wade spoke with a brunette at the front desk of the Wild Prairie Inn.

Their work with the Bureau had required them to stay in a number of cities across the country, and though they had always taken separate rooms, there was nonetheless something intimate in the knowledge that, for as long as the case took, they would be working together throughout the day and then sleeping in the same building every night, next door or across the hall from each other.

She tried to keep her face blank as Wade crossed the carpeted floor toward her, a pair of keys dangling in his hand. He tossed one to her, and she caught it out of the air.

"We can drop off our things in our rooms," he said, "then head to HQ. Sound good?"

She nodded, adjusting her backpack as she headed toward the stairs.

"Where are you going?" Wade asked, gesturing at the elevators.

"When you're used to the great outdoors, shutting yourself in a metal box with a group of strangers doesn't hold much appeal."

Wade chuckled. "Suit yourself. See you in a few."

Piper climbed the stairs, her body—conditioned by the rugged conditions of the Alaska wilderness—showing no fatigue at the climb. It felt good to stretch a little after sitting so long on the plane. She had always been a fan of physical challenges, whether it was hiking up a mountain or chasing down a suspect. It gave her a sense of control, a feeling that she could handle whatever came her way.

When she reached the landing between the third and fourth floors, she paused for a moment to look out the window, studying the broad, broken countryside beyond the edge of the city, all of it covered with a blanket of snow. It might have lacked the jagged peaks of Alaska, but there was something wild and pristine about it nonetheless, a world of mystery waiting to be explored.

Returning to her climb, she reached the fourth floor and moved down the hallway, studying the room numbers. She passed a gaggle of teenagers, their laughter shrill in the narrow passageway. She unlocked her door and hurriedly stepped inside, closing it behind her.

It was a nice room, spacious and clean, with a large window that looked out over the parking lot. There was a king-sized bed with crisp white sheets, a big-screen TV, and a mini-fridge stocked with drinks and snacks.

Despite all these amenities, however, it paled in comparison to the comfort and familiarity of her cabin back in Alaska. Still, it would do for now.

She dropped her backpack on the bed and went to the window, peering out at the sun dipping toward the horizon. The seven-hour flight had chewed up most of the daylight, and it would be dark within a few hours.

All the more reason to head to HQ and get started, she thought.

Still, she hesitated. She couldn't help feeling a little overwhelmed by the thought of entering that room full of strangers, listening to their theories and suggestions and plans of action. She needed some time to do her own investigating, get her own thoughts straight before meeting with the task force.

There was a knock on the door. She opened it to find Wade standing there, eyebrows raised expectantly.

"Ready to get going?" he asked.

She bit her lip. "About that." She paused, unsure where to begin.

Wade sighed, smiling with a look of infinite patience. "Nothing wrong with having the jitters. But as soon as we get started, I promise—"

"It's not that. I just want to have a chance to come to my own conclusions, you know? Before I hear everyone else's ideas."

"We were on that plane for seven hours, Piper. How much time you need?"

He had a point. Still, she sensed she was missing something important. She wanted to at least have a working theory before meeting with the task force, if only so she wouldn't have to go there empty-handed.

"One hour," she said. "Just help me do some research for one hour."

Wade shook his head, suddenly grinning. "I forgot. You don't even have a phone, do you?"

"Technology's not exactly my friend."

He sighed, consulted his watch, and glanced both ways down the hall. Then, after this show of indecision, he stepped into the room and closed the door behind him.

"One hour," he said. "Then we head over there."

Piper felt a flush of gratitude. "Thanks, Wade. Really."

"Clock is ticking, partner. You want to spend that time thanking me or figuring this thing out?"

She retreated a few steps and began pacing across the room. Wade watched her, looking half-amused.

"Still the Energizer Bunny, I see," he said.

She ignored the comment. "I've been thinking about the witness statements. One of them claimed to have seen the kidnapper changing a tire, right?"

He nodded cautiously. "Right."

"I think it was a ruse. That was how he got Vanessa close—he lured her over, probably asking for help, and then he subdued her and dragged her into the van."

Wade rubbed thoughtfully at his goatee. "It's a working theory, I'll give you that."

"That's not the work of an amateur."

Wade's eyes narrowed as he studied her. "What are you saying, Pip? Spit it out."

She took a deep breath and let it out slowly, hoping she was wrong but convinced she was right. "I'm saying," she said, "I don't think this is our kidnapper's first rodeo. I think he's done this before."

CHAPTER FOUR

"Let's not jump to conclusions here," Wade said, his voice laced with caution. "We don't have any concrete evidence to support that theory."

Piper turned to face him, her eyes glinting with determination. "I know it's a bold assumption, but think about it. The way he executed the kidnapping was too precise, too calculated. He knew exactly what he was doing, and he did it with ease. That level of skill doesn't just happen overnight."

Wade pondered her words for a moment before nodding slowly. "Okay, I see your point. But even if he has done this before, we still don't know who he is or where he's hiding."

"I'm getting to that." She went on pacing, her shoes nearly soundless against the carpet. It felt strange to be walking on carpet instead of rough-hewn floorboards.

"If I'm right," she continued, "then there could be cold cases with the same MO. Less sophisticated, maybe, since it probably took time to develop his methods."

"Sophisticated?" Wade repeatedly skeptically. "He pretended to change a tire. That doesn't take a Ph.D."

"No," she agreed, "but it does take a measure of deviousness. Many kidnappers don't set out to kidnap their victims the first time. Usually they try something less sinister—hitting on a hitchhiker, for instance—and only when they're rejected do they take matters into their own hands."

Wade said nothing. He seemed to be considering her words.

Piper, convinced she was on the right track, stopped pacing and frowned at him. "Where would they have those cases on file?"

Wade fished his phone from his pocket and held it up. "Right here, partner. It's called the cloud."

This puzzled Piper. Even before leaving the Bureau a year earlier, she had never been very literate when it came to technology. That was one of the consequences of roughing it in the wild—that, and having a paranoid father who always worried about being tracked.

"I know what the cloud is," she said, annoyed. "But I thought you needed a landline to access the database."

He shook his head. “Not anymore. It’s all right here.”

Piper joined Wade and peered over his shoulder as he typed a few keywords into the search bar. The screen filled with a list of cold cases, each one with its own file number and summary of the crime.

“Let’s start with the ones that match our kidnapper’s MO,” she said as Wade scrolled through the list. “Yellow RV, single female victim, no witnesses.”

“Could’ve changed vehicles by now, if he’s been doing this for a while,” Wade said.

Piper considered this for a moment, then shook her head. “Based on our witness’s description, it sounds like the RV was already a few decades old, maybe from the nineties or even the eighties. My guess is he’s sticking with what he knows, what’s worked for him in the past.”

Wade stopped scrolling and looked at her. “You think he’s sentimental about some old, broke-ass RV?”

“I think he’s sentimental about his method,” she replied, meeting his gaze. “It’s like a signature. He wants to relive the same experience with every victim.”

Wade grunted, the corners of his mouth turning down as if to suggest Piper had hit on something interesting.

They continued to sift through the files, reading through the details of each one. Some they ruled out quickly—the victim was male, too young, or too old; or the vehicle was a bus rather than an RV. Others, however, had eerie similarities to the case they were currently working on.

“This one,” Piper said, pointing. “It’s from two years ago.” She began summarizing as she read. “A young woman, college student, disappeared while hiking alone in the mountains. Witnesses saw a yellow RV parked near the trailhead that day, but no one thought to take down the license plate.”

She paused, her stomach sinking. “The victim’s body was found a month later, deep in the wilderness. She’d been murdered.”

Wade’s face darkened as he read through the details. “This sounds like our guy, all right. Same vehicle, lone female victim, no witnesses. Let’s see if there are any others.”

As they continued to search the database, it quickly became apparent that their unsub—Bureau-speak for “unknown subject”—might very well be responsible for a number of similar murders over the years, ranging in location from Wyoming, Montana, Minnesota, and all the way up into Canada. Even though the dump sites were many miles apart, they all had one thing in common: They were extremely remote.

"Looks like this bearded bastard likes the wilderness," Wade said with a disgusted shake of his head.

Piper clenched her jaw. "That's where he feels safe. It's his element, where he can do what he wants far from prying eyes."

They continued searching through the files, hoping to find something that could lead them to their suspect. As they worked, Piper's mind began to wander. She thought back to her teenage years when she roamed about with her father, spending her days tracking animals through the dense forests and using her intuition and knowledge of the land to find her way. Now she was tracking a different kind of predator, a creature far more devious than any animal.

A creature that, if cornered, would almost certainly strike back.

After a while Piper's eyes grew tired of staring at the screen, and she retreated to the window, watching the sun sink steadily toward the horizon. It was not even six o'clock, but already the light had a fragile quality to it, as if it might shatter at any moment.

Wade sighed deeply and tossed his phone onto the bed. He sat down, and the mattress echoed back his sigh.

"Most of those women haven't even been found," he said, his voice heavy with frustration. "We have no idea how many bodies are out there."

Piper shook her head, her eyes still fixed on the horizon. "No, but we know enough to start putting together a profile. We know his preferred method, his preferred location, and his preferred target. And, maybe best of all, we know about his vehicle."

Even as she spoke the words, she found herself battling a sense of hopelessness. Their unsub had been doing this for years, preying on young women at will and getting away with it. What made her think they could stop him when so many others had failed?

But she couldn't let herself give in to that kind of thinking. As an agent, she had to believe that justice could be served, that she and Wade could catch this killer and put him behind bars.

For Vanessa's sake, yes, but also for the sakes of all those other women he had killed.

As the sun slipped behind the horizon, Piper took a bracing breath and turned around. "Come on," she said softly. "We'd better meet with the task force, let them know what we've found. Vanessa might still be alive..."

She paused, her words lingering in the air. “But judging by our unsub’s past behavior, she may not have much time left.”

CHAPTER FIVE

Yes, Jake thought, navigating the winding road as it led deep into North Dakota's rugged wilderness, *she has to be the one.*

Peering into the rearview mirror, he could see the two women stretched out like rolled-up carpets, one on the floor and one across the seats. The one on the floor, her limbs tied together and her mouth covered with duct tape, had a name that started with M—Madge, he thought, or maybe Marge. He couldn't remember. He had stalked her for two full weeks before finally snatching her from a gas station in a small town on the outskirts of Fargo.

The other woman, the one sprawled across the seats, was Vanessa. She had woken while he was tying her up, begging him to let her go, explaining how her father was the governor and would pay him handsomely for her return. He'd laughed inwardly at this, amused by her desperate attempts.

She was unconscious now—he had choked her out, careful to make sure he did not deprive her of oxygen for too long—and he stared at her, watching her head loll against the window as the RV bounced along the rutted road.

Jake couldn't help but chuckle to himself as he thought about the irony of his situation. He, who had spent so much time alone in the wilderness, now had two women captive in his mobile home. It was almost too easy. The first, Madge or Marge or whatever her name was, had put up a bit of a struggle, but in the end, Jake had easily overpowered her. Vanessa had been even easier.

More innocent, more unsuspecting.

He reached for the bottle of water resting in the cup holder and took a long swig. The sun had set behind the mountains, and the sky was a deep shade of blue-black. The stars were just beginning to twinkle into view, and the only sounds were the rumble of the RV's engine and the occasional howl of a coyote.

Jake was in his element. He had been stalking women like these two for years, perfecting his method, growing ever more efficient. He was good at this.

Too good, one might say.

After all, he had never intended to pick up Vanessa in the first place. He'd been in town to gather supplies, and he only stopped at the school to stretch his legs. But as soon as he saw her walking into the school, her blonde hair shining in the sun, he'd known she had to be his.

After that, it was a simple matter of making a show of changing a tire. She'd come over to help, dutiful young lady that she was, and he'd plucked her as easily as a ripe apple from a low-hanging branch.

Now here he was, driving deep into the wilderness with his two captives in tow. He had everything he needed in his RV—food, water, tools, restraints, weapons. He had planned everything out to the minutest detail.

The only problem was…he'd only planned on having one guest, not two. Everything would be far more difficult with two.

The solution's simple, then, he thought. *You'll just have to kill one of them.*

Yes, that was the logical thing to do. But even as he considered the idea, he couldn't help feeling a twinge of guilt. Could he really kill one of these two without even giving her the chance to prove herself? Was he really capable of that?

Jake had not always been this way. Once upon a time he had been helpless himself—a victim to society's expectations, society's prejudices. He'd been an outcast, forced to fend for himself when other kids were being coddled by protective, understanding parents. And for a long time, he'd accepted this as his identity.

Something changed, however, with the first hitchhiker. She was a young woman, a college girl who'd been out celebrating with her friends. Jake had picked her up on a deserted stretch of highway, and as soon as she was settled in the passenger seat, he knew what he had to do. It was like a switch had been flipped inside him; suddenly he was in control, and she was at his mercy.

He had never felt so powerful, so alive.

Nothing was the same after that first time. He now understood that he did not have to ask for what he wanted—he could simply take it. He had embraced his new identity as a predator, as someone who could control and manipulate those weaker than him.

But could he control his own impulses? That was the question that plagued him now. He knew he had to make a decision soon, before the situation spiraled out of control.

As he drove deeper into the wilderness, he became aware of a growing sense of unease. Was it his conscience, finally rearing its ugly head? Or was it something else, something more primal and dangerous?

Jake couldn't be sure, but he knew one thing for certain: He had to be careful. One wrong move, one slip-up, and everything he had worked for would come crashing down around him.

He turned his attention back to the road, his grip tightening on the steering wheel. The RV bounced over a particularly rough patch of terrain, and the two women moaned softly in their sleep.

He thought of the brochure he had found in Vanessa's pocket, the one about the so-called Green Rights bill. She cared about the environment, that much was clear. But did she really understand what such words meant? Could she love the wilderness even when it was bitter and bleak, when the wind howled and the snow fell in thick, blinding flakes? Could she survive out here on her own if she had to, or was she just a spoiled little rich girl talking about things she couldn't understand?

Only one way to find out. You'll know the answer soon enough. There's no lying, not out here.

She would get her chance. And Marge—well, Marge might just be a casualty of poor timing. Jake was still not sure what he intended to do. He would play it by ear, see how they each reacted when they woke up.

Dimly, in the back of his mind, he was aware of the very real possibility that neither of these two women would prove to be the one he was looking for. That would be disappointing, but if it happened, it happened.

There were plenty of fish in the sea.

With a sense of determination, Jake pressed down harder on the gas pedal, eager to reach his destination. He had work to do, and he couldn't afford any distractions. He had to remain focused if he was going to succeed.

And he would succeed. This time, he felt certain, he had finally found the one he was looking for.

CHAPTER SIX

The chattering of voices hit Piper like a physical force as Wade opened the door, ushering her into the room that was functioning as the task force's headquarters.

The room was situated on the second floor of Governor Johnston's home. A long rosewood table ran down the center, surrounded by chairs, with a large screen on one wall displaying a map of the region. A number of agents and local law enforcement officers were scattered around the room, some talking on phones or typing on laptops, others huddled in small groups, discussing the case.

Piper froze, feeling an uncomfortable crawling sensation on the nape of her neck, as if a spider were patrolling across her skin. She found herself wondering why she had ever thought it was a good idea to leave the safety and familiarity of her remote cabin.

Gradually, the voices of the other officials fell silent as they turned their gaze to the newcomers. Piper felt like an insect under a magnifying glass. To her relief, Wade spared her from having to introduce herself.

"Governor Johnston," he said, "this is Piper Woods, the tracker I was telling you about."

A man in a crisp suit, his gray-streaked hair smoothed back from his forehead, crossed the room toward them. Stubble the color of ash was breaking out across his face, and his eyes had a haggard, drooping look to them that suggested he'd gotten little—if any—sleep the previous night.

I wouldn't be sleeping either, Piper thought. *Not if my daughter had just been kidnapped.*

"Wade tells me you're the best," Johnston said, extending his hand. "I hope you can help us find my daughter."

Piper clasped his hand tightly, trying to convey a sense of confidence and determination. "I'll do everything in my power to bring her home, sir," she said firmly.

Johnston nodded, his eyes heavy with emotion. "You won't be alone. We've got the best and brightest here." Despite his words, Piper sensed a hint of exasperation in his tone, as if he didn't feel the investigation was proceeding as quickly as he had hoped.

He cleared his throat and gestured toward the table. "Well, why don't you share your thoughts with the group? I'm sure Lawrence has caught you up to speed."

Lawrence. Wade hated being called by his first name, as Piper knew. He thought it sounded prissy, the name of a country gentleman, which was why he went by his last name instead. The only exception to this was his nickname, "the Law," given to him during training at Quantico for being a hardass nobody wanted to cross. He had mellowed out somewhat since then, but he could still be a bear when roused.

Piper swallowed hard as the silence in the room deepened. She felt the weight of all their expectations bearing down on her. Composing herself with an effort, she took a deep breath and stepped forward.

"We've been going over the cold cases in the police database," she began, her voice steady. "And we've found a number of similarities between our current case and a string of unsolved murders scattered across several states and Canada."

"How do you know they're linked?" a man with a gruff voice interrupted, his arms folded across his chest. He was wearing the uniform of a U.S. marshal.

"Because the MO is the same," Piper replied without hesitation. "The victims were all young women, and their bodies were found in remote wilderness areas. Our unsub seems to have a preference for the outdoors."

"He's a hunter," Wade added, his voice low. "And he knows how to use the terrain to his advantage."

The marshal nodded, his eyes growing thoughtful. "Any other ties between the cases?"

"The yellow RV," Piper said, grateful he'd asked. "It's been seen in the vicinity of all the murder sites."

A state police officer—the gold bar on his uniform read "ROBERT TENNY"—spoke up. "We've interviewed dozens of Bakerfield students, but nobody recalls seeing the plate. It does appear, though, that the vehicle in question is a Volkswagen camper van, probably from the seventies or eighties."

"How versatile are those?" Governor Johnston asked. Piper knew immediately what he was getting at. He wanted to know how far the killer might take his daughter into the wilderness, how far off the beaten path he could get.

Tenny made a skeptical face. "Not very, especially not in snow. He won't stray far from paved roads."

As much as Piper wanted to avoid the spotlight, she found herself contradicting Tenny anyway. "I'm not sure that's true," she said.

The room fell silent again. Tenny raised an imperious eyebrow at her. "Beg pardon?"

She cleared her throat. "This kidnapper doesn't keep his victims close to civilization, not even close to established roads. He takes them deep into the wilderness, where nobody can get at him."

"And how, pray tell, would he do that in a camper van?"

Piper glanced at Wade. He nodded encouragingly as if to say, *Go on. Don't be shy.*

She shrugged one shoulder. "My guess? He hides the van, then takes another vehicle—an ATV, maybe. Something that can handle off-road terrain and narrow trails."

Governor Johnston leaned forward, his eyes glinting with renewed hope. "Do you have any idea where he might have hidden the van?"

Piper shook her head. "Not yet. He might have covered it with a tarp, or camouflaged it with branches and leaves. We'll have to search the area thoroughly."

Wade chimed in. "We're going to need more manpower and resources. We need to bring in search dogs, drones, and all-terrain vehicles."

Governor Johnston nodded. "Consider it done. We'll mobilize everything we've got."

"We need to move fast," Piper added, trying to inject a renewed sense of urgency into the room. "Based on his previous history, our unsub probably hasn't strayed far from the kidnapping site. We need to map out the area, start checking security cameras and speaking with residents to see if anyone's seen an RV that fits our description."

She wanted to add that Vanessa might not have long to live, but considering the fact that the missing girl's father was in the room, she bit her lip and kept that to herself for the moment. There was no need to focus on the worst possible outcome or to cause the governor unnecessary pain.

A grizzled man with a military-style haircut, seated to the right of the governor, spoke up. "If the kidnapper has a lick of common sense," he said, "he'll get as far from that college as possible before we can start setting up checkpoints. We need to widen our search, not narrow it."

Piper shook her head. "That doesn't fit the pattern of the previous kidnappings. He's not worried about checkpoints because he sticks to the wilderness as much as possible."

The man looked around, frowning in confusion. "I'm sorry, why are you here again? Aren't you the one who let that serial killer get away? From what I hear, you really cracked—left the Bureau and became a hermit up in Alaska, didn't you?"

The room went suddenly silent. Piper felt a flush creeping up her neck. She had known that her sudden appearance in the case would raise some eyebrows, but she hadn't expected to be called out so openly and so personally.

Wade stepped forward, his face tense. "Agent Woods has an impressive track record in missing persons cases, including several high-profile ones. She's the real deal, and she can help us find the governor's daughter."

The man didn't look convinced. "I don't care who vouches for her. If I'm the kidnapper, I'm avoiding that college like the plague, not sticking around so I can get caught. I want to know why Agent Woods here thinks she knows better."

Piper swallowed hard, feeling the weight of the man's scrutiny like a physical presence. She knew she needed to say something, to prove that she was worthy of being here, but her mind was blank.

"Well?" he said. "Are you going to answer or just stand there?"

"I've been tracking missing persons for over a decade," she said at last, her voice coming out harder and more brittle than she'd intended. "I know the wilderness, and what it takes to survive out there even in the midst of harsh winter conditions—how to build a fire with wet fuel, how to find food in the wild, how to navigate without a map or GPS. And I know how to find someone who doesn't want to be found."

The man snorted. "From what I understand, that's all you've been doing for the past year—surviving, roughing it in the bush. But I'm afraid this isn't some cagey bear we're after, sweetheart. He's a deviant criminal, the kind most of us deal with on a daily basis." He looked around at the other faces at the table. There were a few nods.

"So why don't you leave the criminology to the experts?" he suggested in a tone that was anything but a suggestion. "When the government decides to hunt down Bigfoot, we'll be sure to call you."

This was the exact thing Piper had feared—that she would be brought back just to hear her views discounted, minimized, dismissed. She was used to fighting an uphill battle—that was part of being a female agent in a male-dominated field—but this felt different. This was personal. She didn't want to be seen as some amateurish survivalist who thought she knew more than the police.

Piper took a deep breath and glared at the man. "I understand that some of you have more experience in dealing with criminals than I do," she said, "but you don't know the wilderness like I do. I grew up in this terrain, and I know how to track suspects through it. I know how to find someone who doesn't want to be found. And I won't rest until we find the governor's daughter. So we can either keep wasting our time questioning my skills, or we can work together to save the governor's daughter."

The words were out before she could stop them. *Now you've done it,* she thought. *They'll send you packing for sure.*

She waited with bated breath, wondering what would happen now. There was a stunned silence in the room. Governor Johnston gave her a small smile of support, but most of the other officials were looking at her in surprise.

Wade put a hand on her shoulder, a silent warning to keep her cool. "Gentlemen, let's not lose sight of the task at hand," he said, his voice carrying a note of authority. "We need to focus on finding the governor's daughter, and we need to do it quickly. Agent Woods has given us some valuable insights into the case, and we should consider ourselves lucky to have her on our team."

The grizzled man merely grunted and rose. "Just so long as she stays out of my way," he said in a low voice, "we won't have any problems."

With that, he strode out of the room, leaving a palpable tension behind. Piper let out a breath she hadn't realized she'd been holding. She could feel the eyes of the other officials on her, assessing and judging.

Governor Johnston cleared his throat. "Well then, let's get started. I want to learn everything we can about this RV."

Wade nodded, gesturing to a state map hanging on the wall. "In the previous kidnappings," he said, "the unsub never strayed more than fifty miles or so from the site of the kidnapping."

Piper couldn't help noticing how careful Wade was not to mention anything about murder. He spoke only of kidnapping, as if those previous women hadn't been found dead. Piper understood his reasoning, of course—she didn't want to be the one to tell Johnston his daughter probably wouldn't be alive much longer, either.

Grabbing a pencil from the table, Wade drew a large circle around Bakerfield University.

"I suggest we divide this into sectors," he continued, "and assign a team to each."

“Like slices of pie,” Johnston said.

Wade nodded. “That’s right. Agent Woods and I will take one, and she’ll use her experience in tracking and survival to cover the more rugged terrain. The rest of you can search the more populated areas.”

There were murmurs of agreement around the table, and Piper felt a small sense of relief. Maybe they were willing to give her a chance, after all.

As the officials began to divvy up the sectors, Piper leaned in closer to Wade. “Thanks for backing me up,” she said quietly.

Wade gave her a small smile. “Of course. What are partners for?”

Piper felt a warmth spreading through her chest at the compliment. It was good to know that at least one person in the room trusted her.

“Who *was* that guy, anyway?” she asked.

“The one who looked ready to chew you up and spit you out? That’s Carl Aiken. He’s a private security contractor the governor brought in—old friend of the family. Governor Johnston trusts him with his life.”

Piper frowned. “Aiken sure doesn’t seem like a fan of mine.”

Wade chuckled. “He’s not a fan of anyone who isn’t him. He’s got some kind of chip on his shoulder about law enforcement. Thinks he knows better than anyone else.”

Piper raised an eyebrow. “And yet he’s working with the governor’s office?”

Wade shrugged. “Politics, I suppose. He’s got connections, and he’s good at what he does. But don’t let him get to you. You know what you’re doing. And we’re going to find that RV and bring the governor’s daughter home.”

Piper nodded, grateful for her partner’s confidence in her. She made a mental note to steer clear of Aiken as much as possible.

Wade lifted his jacket from the chair he had draped it across and threw it over his shoulders. “Come on,” he said to Piper. “Let’s go get our gear and head out. We’ve got a lot of ground to cover.”

As they stepped outside, Piper glimpsed a blur of movement to her right. She barely had time to react before a hand gripped her shoulder and Aiken’s face loomed before her, pale and furious in the weak light.

“Don’t you ever embarrass me like that again,” he said in a harsh whisper, “or I’ll bury you, understand?”

Piper stared at him, surprised by the venom in his voice. Wade had moved on ahead without noticing Aiken, but now he turned around and stared at them, looking puzzled. Before he could ask what was going on, however, Aiken moved away, smiling now.

"Good luck, Agent Woods," he said, no longer whispering. "Be careful out there—it's so easy to have an accident in the dark, isn't it?"

CHAPTER SEVEN

"You sure we're not lost?" Wade asked, glancing across the cabin of the SUV at Piper, who sat in the passenger seat with a map spread in her lap. The dome light was on, and she was tracing their route with her finger, her eyebrows knitted together in concentration.

"We should be close to the trailhead now," she said, ignoring her partner's question. "It's closed for the season, but that's not going to stop our unsub."

The SUV bounced as they hit a pothole, and Piper glanced up, studying the snow-clad trees framing the road. The temperature was dropping by the hour, and she was grateful they'd taken the time to pick up some wilderness gear from a local outfitter before heading out. The last thing they needed was to get stuck in the middle of nowhere without proper clothing or supplies.

"We're almost there," she said, pointing to a signpost up ahead. "Take a left at the next junction, and we should hit the trailhead in a mile or so."

Wade nodded, turning the SUV onto the smaller road. The headlights bounced off the trees, casting eerie shadows on the snow. In her mind, Piper found herself planning how they would make camp, if necessary: where they would build their shelter, what materials they might use for fire, how they would keep warm.

Keeping herself warm, of course, was not the real challenge. She was used to the cold, used to waking every few hours to load the stove so that the temperature in her cabin didn't plummet into the teens—or lower. Wade, on the other hand, was a city boy, used to central heating and never straying far from urban areas. She couldn't help but feel a twinge of amusement at the thought of him struggling to keep up with her in the wilderness.

But now was not the time for jokes. They were on a mission, and her focus needed to be sharp. The governor's daughter was out there somewhere, cold and scared and in danger. Piper couldn't let herself rest until she found her.

As they pulled up to the trailhead, Piper scanned the parking lot, searching for any signs of the RV. The lot, however, was deserted, the trail closed off by a gate secured with a rusted padlock.

"I don't see any tracks," Wade said, stopping the vehicle. "Where to next?"

Piper, however, was not so eager to move on. "When did it snow last?" she asked.

"This morning, I think." Understanding dawned in his eyes. "You think he might've gone up the trail into the park sometime last night?"

"I think we'd better check that lock and see if it's been tampered with."

Wade nodded, grabbing his flashlight from the glove compartment. The two agents stepped out of the SUV and approached the gate, the crunching of snow beneath their boots the only sound in the silent forest.

Piper knelt down and examined the lock. "It's been cut," she said, feeling both troubled and excited as she stood back up. "The RV could be anywhere by now."

Wade cursed under his breath. "Let's get this gate open."

Piper hesitated, studying the snow. "It's too deep," she said. "We won't make it far, not through these drifts."

She realized the snowfall had been heavy, either during the night or perhaps that morning. The RV could have come through the previous day, when the trail was more navigable, and its tracks would have been completely covered. Now the snow reached almost to Piper's knees, and she knew there was little chance of getting far in the SUV.

There was only one option.

"We have to go on foot," she said.

Wade groaned. "Are you serious? We'll freeze to death out here."

"Not if we're careful. We'll have to move slowly, making sure we don't sweat. That's the bigger danger right now—chilling ourselves with our own sweat."

It was clear from the agonized look on Wade's face that he didn't like this plan. Piper punched him playfully on the shoulder. "Come on, tough guy," she said. "I thought you grew up in Detroit. Winters must get pretty cold there."

"Not like this," he said, slapping his gloved hands together. "The way I figure, winter's good for pictures. The only snow I like is the kind I see out the window while I'm relaxing in a hot tub."

Piper couldn't help but smile, despite the circumstances.

They returned to the vehicle to grab their gear. Piper slipped on her backpack, which contained all the essentials they would need for a few nights in the wilderness: first aid kit, fire-making tools, a pot for boiling water, a sleeping bag, meal packs, a small stove, and a number of smaller items. She also grabbed a few nutrition bars from the console of the car and tucked them into her pocket.

Wade, meanwhile, pulled on his own backpack, grumbling as he did so. "I hope you know what you're doing," he said to Piper. "I don't want to end up as a frozen statue out here."

Piper rolled her eyes. "Get moving, tough guy. We've got a daughter to find."

With that, the two agents set off on foot into the snowy wilderness. The cold air was invigorating, and Piper felt her senses sharpening with each passing step. She was in her element now, and nothing could stop her from finding the missing woman.

As they hiked, the snow grew deeper, reaching above their knees in some places. Piper led the way, pausing occasionally to consult her map.

Wade chuckled as he caught up with her. "Still can't believe you use that thing," he said, shaking his head. "Ever heard of GPS?"

Piper's distrust of technology ran deep, imprinted on her by years spent with her father. Luke Woods had been distrustful of technology as far back as Piper could remember, always suspecting someone was listening in or watching their every move. He'd also taught her that over-reliance on technology blunted one's skills, leaving a person helpless if a phone or computer should stop working.

"You never know when technology will fail you," she said, glancing up at the snow-covered trees. "If you lose signal, your GPS stops working. But a map will always work, so long as you keep it with you."

Wade shrugged, his breath misting in the cold air. "Suit yourself," he said. "I just prefer the easy way."

The trail led them deep into the wilderness, with no light except the glow of their flashlights. The sky was overcast, and heavy flakes drifted lazily through the air, just thick enough to compromise visibility. Piper was grateful for the heavy boots she wore, as they kept her feet dry and warm.

"Watch out for widowmakers," she said, interrupting the rhythmic hissing of their boots sinking into the snow.

"Widowmakers?"

She gestured up at a broken branch three or four inches in diameter suspended precariously at the top of one of the trees. "If the wind picks up and one of those comes down on you, you'll never be heard from again."

Wade grunted. "Thanks for the warning."

They went on in silence awhile longer. Then Wade said, "I've gotta admit, I didn't think you'd come back. You seemed pretty snug out there in your Alaska cabin."

At first, Piper didn't answer. She just kept staring ahead at the path, unsure what to say.

"Pip?" Wade said.

"I guess I've got a savior complex."

It was not much of an answer, and she could tell by Wade's silence that he knew this. She suspected he knew her better than she realized. She didn't know whether this was reassuring or unsettling.

"That's not really the reason, is it?" Wade said quietly. "You know you have to stop beating yourself up for what happened to Fiona, right?"

Piper bit her lip, feeling suddenly vulnerable, exposed, as if a secret she was desperately trying to hide had just been dragged into the light. He was right, of course—her guilt for Fiona's death was a big part of her reason for agreeing to join the task force and help rescue Governor Johnston's daughter. But that didn't mean she was ready to talk about it.

Several moments passed in silence. Then Wade said, "It wasn't your fault. What Gray did to her, I mean. Gray was a monster, and if it hadn't been Fiona, he would have hurt someone else."

Piper felt her throat tighten at the mention of Gray's name. Why, after all this time, could she still recall his face with such sharp clarity? Had he burrowed somehow into the folds of her brain, hiding there like a grub to slowly devour her?

"I know that," she said, her voice tight. "You don't have to tell me how evil he was."

"So why are you punishing yourself for his crimes?"

She stopped and turned to face him, anger and grief warring within her. "I don't want to talk about this, okay?" she said. "Not here, not now. Understand?"

He nodded slowly. There was a look of sadness in his eyes, as if he had just suffered some personal loss. "Okay, Pip," he said quietly. "Okay."

They continued on in silence, their pace slowing as the snow grew even deeper. It was a grueling hike, with each step becoming more exhausting than the last. Piper pushed on relentlessly, punishing her body to keep herself from thinking of Gray or Fiona or anything but the present moment.

They crested a hill, and on the other side Piper could see the glow of a campfire burning in a small hollow. Several figures were gathered around it, bearded men in camouflage with beers in their hands and tents set up behind them. Several ATVs stood nearby, along with a tarp on which lay the carcass of an elk. Two men were busy butchering the animal, one cutting with the knife while the other laid strips of meat in a pan.

Just in time for dinner, Piper thought.

"I don't see an RV anywhere," Wade said in a low voice, clicking off his flashlight so as to avoid giving away their position. "I wonder if these guys are the ones who clipped the lock on the gate."

"If they are," Piper answered softly, "they may not be thrilled to see us. This park is public land, and judging by the locked gate, I'm guessing they didn't get permission to hunt here."

Wade nodded, his eyes scanning the scene before them. "Probably armed to the teeth, too. Want to hang tight, call in backup in case this gets messy?"

Piper considered this, then shook her head. "We don't have that kind of time. I think we can handle this on our own, don't you?"

Wade took a deep, hesitant breath. "Nobody lives forever, right? So how are you thinking of doing this?"

"We'll get close, listen to see whether they say anything about Vanessa or a yellow RV."

"And if they do?"

Piper clenched her jaw. "Then we'll have a few questions for them. Now stick close behind me, and do exactly as I do."

Taking advantage of the darkness, Piper crept forward, keeping her body low to the ground as she approached the camp. The snow made it difficult to move quietly, but she did her best, taking slow, deliberate steps.

As she drew nearer, Piper could hear the men talking. Their voices were rough and gruff, their laughter sounding like the braying of donkeys. They were drunk, that much was clear.

Sensing the firelight would give them away if they got any closer, Piper motioned for Wade to crouch. Then she held a finger to her lips. As she listened, two of the men began arguing about which of them had fired the shot that killed the elk.

"Come on, Marty," a man with beady little eyes and a paunch said. "You know you can't shoot for shit. That was my bullet that hit the deer. You just scared it off with your damn coughing fit."

"You're full of it, Frank," Marty retorted, taking a swig of his beer. "I'm the best shot here, and you know it."

Piper exchanged a look with Wade. He rolled his eyes.

"Best at drinking shots, maybe," Frank answered.

At this, Marty rose unsteadily, reaching for the shotgun leaning against his chair. He pointed it at his friend with a drunken grin. "I'll show you who can't shoot," he slurred.

Piper cursed under her breath. This was getting out of hand, and they needed to act fast before someone got hurt. Acting on instincts honed from her many hours of training in the Bureau, Piper drew her sidearm and rose in one smooth motion.

"FBI!" she shouted. "Put down the weapon!"

The men turned as one, their faces rapidly changing from friendly, to baffled, and finally to hostile. Marty pivoted toward them, the shotgun swinging around, and Piper's finger was tightening around the trigger of her own gun when Frank reached out to lower the barrel of the shotgun.

"What are you trying to do?" he growled at Marty. "Get us all killed?"

Marty mumbled something and sank back into his chair, looking sheepish.

"Sorry about that," Frank said, putting his hands up in a gesture of surrender. "We didn't realize we had company. What are you fine folks doing all the way out here?"

Despite the reasonableness in Frank's words, Piper sensed a tension in the air, and she realized she would have to proceed carefully. It seemed clear these men were poachers, but she had very little interest in bringing them in on such a charge, not when her real focus was on finding Vanessa.

"We're looking for a yellow RV," she said. "We saw the broken lock on the gate and thought the vehicle might have come up this way. Have any of you seen a vehicle like that?"

The men exchanged curious glances.

"No," Frank said, shaking his head slowly. "Can't say we have. We've been here for a couple of days and haven't seen a soul. What's in the RV, anyway? A meth lab?"

He said this almost as a joke, though such a thing was far from ridiculous.

"We're looking for a missing person," Piper said, keeping her voice calm. "A young woman named Vanessa. She was kidnapped."

"Well, that's a shame," Frank said. "It's a terrible thing, the way you can get snatched up without warning these days. When I was a kid—" He stopped suddenly, then sat forward. "Wait a minute. Are you talking about Vanessa Johnston? The governor's daughter?"

"Heard about it on the radio," Marty added, his words slightly slurred. "Terrible, terrible thing."

"That's right," Wade said. "The governor's offering a reward of one hundred thousand dollars to anyone who can provide information leading to her rescue."

Frank leaned back, shaking his head wonderingly. "Now I really wish we *had* seen her—not like we wouldn't want to help you find her out of the goodness of our hearts, of course."

Of course, Piper thought, disgusted that this man could have so little compassion for a kidnapped girl. She was about to ask for more information about the area when the radio clipped to Wade's belt crackled to life, the transmission garbled. He raised it to his ear and turned away.

"What's that?" he said in a low voice.

Piper stared at the poachers, who gazed back at her without a hint of friendliness. After a few moments, Wade set a hand on her shoulder and murmured in her ear.

"Just got a hit on a vehicle matching the description," he said in a low voice. "Just north of here, past Starvation Valley. It's not our sector, but—"

"But it's close," Piper murmured back, frowning. "We can get there first if we hoof it."

"What do you say, partner?"

She nodded, coming to a decision. "Let's go. We can report these guys to the local PD, let them know what's going on."

As Piper started away, retracing her footsteps through the snow, Wade raised a hand toward the poachers. "Thanks for the help," he said.

"No problem," Frank answered, his eyes narrowed. "You be careful out there, you hear? The wilderness can be a dangerous place if you're not careful."

CHAPTER EIGHT

"It was called in by a mechanic," Wade said, piloting the SUV along the dark, winding road as Piper once again gave directions. "He has a little side job plowing, and he was on his way home after clearing a few properties. He heard the APB on the radio just a few minutes before he spotted the RV."

"And he's sure it matches the description?" Piper asked, her attention on the map. The last thing they needed was to go off on a wild goose chase. Everyone on the task force, Piper and Wade included, was so eager for a lead that they were ready to snap at anything, like a team of sled dogs at chow time.

"Said he was," Wade answered. "Didn't stick around, though—had his kids with him in the back seats, and he wasn't about to put them in danger."

Piper nodded, still concentrating on the map but occasionally glancing up to study the road. The headlights cut sharply through the darkness, reflecting off banks of snow mounded on either side, above which the trees loomed like sinister sentinels. The forest was not as thick here, however—it was falling away, giving ground to the barren tundra of the northernmost part of the region, a stretch of rolling, broken wilderness hardly disturbed by civilization.

A clearing came into view on the right, and Wade slowed, peering out the window past Piper. It appeared to be a small turnaround, but as far as Piper could tell, it was entirely empty.

"You sure this is right?" Wade asked, leaning over the map.

"According to what he told us, yeah. We're on Skylark Road, and we just passed Herschel's Feed Store. This has got to be it."

Wade leaned back and rubbed his chin, his eyes asking an unspoken question: *Where's the RV, then?*

"Just pull in if you can," Piper said. "I want to take a closer look."

Wade did so, guiding the SUV into the deep snow. After twenty or thirty feet, Piper held up a hand.

"That's far enough," she said. She pointed out the windshield. "You see that pair of faint lines in the snow, almost like shadows?"

Wade leaned forward, squinting as he stared out the window. "I see them, yeah."

"Vehicle tracks," she said, feeling a growing sense of urgency as her instincts stirred within her. "It looks like they head away from us, past those trees. We need to follow them."

Wade nodded. "I'll call it in." He lifted the radio to his mouth. "This is Wade," he said. "We're at the turnaround on Skylark Road. No sign of the RV, but we've got tracks heading into the trees. We're going to follow on foot."

He let go of the button and listened, waiting.

"Aren't you supposed to use code words?" Piper asked, genuinely curious. "In case someone is listening in?"

"Not with these babies," he said, tapping the radio. "Encrypted. No chance of being overheard."

Piper nodded, bewildered as always by the advances in technology. Then a voice came over the radio.

"Wade, this is Aiken. I'll be there in ten."

"We can't wait," Piper said to Wade. "We have to go now."

Wade nodded and lifted the radio again. "Roger that. We're going to head out, all the same. We'll let you know what we find."

"I don't think that's a good idea," Aiken said, sounding slightly frustrated. "You should hang tight until we can reinforce you."

Wade glanced at Piper. She was no mind-reader, so she couldn't have said for certain what Aiken's motives were, but she had the distinct impression he was worried that if they went on ahead without him, they might get all the credit. It seemed clear that it was more important to him to get the credit for rescuing Vanessa than to make sure she was saved at all costs.

Piper gestured for the radio and took it. "This is Piper," she said. "We can't wait—there's no telling how much time Vanessa has left. You can catch up when you're able."

Without waiting for a reply, Piper climbed out of the vehicle. She knew Aiken would be angry, but her focus was not on appeasing a private security contractor, no matter how connected he might be, especially when a life hung in the balance.

Wade said nothing as he joined her, and she was grateful that he didn't chide her or suggest she ought to have been more tactful. He seemed to understand as well as she did what was the priority and what was not.

The tracks were shallow and nearly obscured by the wind-drifted snow, but Piper could still make out the path they'd taken. As she peered down at them, an icy wind struck her, causing her to stiffen.

"Come on," she said. "No time to waste."

She led the way, her senses on high alert as they plodded through the snow, following the faint trail left by the RV. The wilderness was eerily quiet, as if holding its breath in anticipation of something momentous. Piper's heart rate kicked up a notch as they approached a thick clump of trees.

As they stepped into the woods, the snow became deeper, and Piper found herself having to push through drifts that reached up past her knees. She glanced over her shoulder and saw that Wade was having no better luck. Despite the difficulty, however, he showed no signs of quitting. His face was grim and set with determination.

"I ever tell you," he said between breaths, "how much I hate the cold?"

"A time or two," she answered.

They pushed on for what felt like hours, though Piper doubted it had been more than twenty minutes. Finally, they broke through the trees and found themselves on a rocky outcropping that overlooked a wide expanse of frozen tundra. The tracks wound around to their left, but Piper decided to use the outcropping to survey the terrain ahead.

"See anything?" Wade asked, leaning on his knees to catch his breath.

At first the tundra appeared to be empty, nearly featureless beneath the blanket of snow. Then, peering downward, she saw the RV perhaps a hundred feet below them, light glowing from the windows. Seeing it, Piper felt a rush of excitement.

"It's there," she whispered to Wade. "Right below us."

He peered over the edge, a queasy look on his face. "I ever tell you I hate heights, too?"

Piper was too focused on the mission for banter. "We have to get down there. We can descend the rocks here—that way, if the kidnapper's watching for anyone following his trail, he won't see us."

Wade gave the slope, which pitched downward at a forty-five-degree angle, a dubious look. "That's going to be treacherous in the snow," he said.

Piper nodded, her eyes scanning the area around the RV. "But we have no choice. The RV might be stuck there, but that doesn't mean they are. The kidnapper could have a snowmobile, or he could even grab Vanessa and head out on foot. The longer we hesitate, the worse Vanessa's chances become."

With a deep breath, she started down the slope, using the rocks as footholds. The snow was deep here too, and it was slow going, each step feeling like a potential disaster.

Slow your breathing, she reminded herself, recalling the advice her father had given her over the years as they stalked wild game in the Alaska wilderness. One of his favorite sayings, an aphorism he had learned from a Navy Seal, came back to Piper: *Slow is smooth, smooth is fast.*

She was halfway down the slope when Wade gave a muffled cry behind her. He came stumbling forward, unable to slow himself, and Piper reached out to grab him, her fingers clutching onto his arm and helping him get his balance.

"Didn't want to show off, make it look too easy," he said in a hushed voice, offering a queasy smile.

"Of course not," Piper agreed.

Despite the joke, Piper had no illusions as to the danger they were facing. The slope was slick with snow and ice, and one wrong step could easily lead to a broken leg—or worse. But they couldn't give up now, not when they were so close.

Together, they continued down the slope, their breaths coming in ragged gasps. The RV grew larger and larger as they approached, until finally they were crouched behind a boulder just a few feet away from it.

Piper could hear voices coming from inside, muffled and indistinct. Her heart pounded in her chest, and sweat trickled down her back beneath her heavy coat.

"The textbook thing to do would be to call it in and wait for backup," Wade said. Despite the words, however, Piper could tell from his tone that he didn't really want to do this. He seemed to want the same thing she did: to move ahead while they had the element of surprise, rather than waiting for backup and potentially forfeiting this opportunity.

She was about to say so when she heard the distinct sound of an approaching engine. Alarmed, she glanced to the left to see several snowmobiles approaching, zipping down the slope toward the RV.

Aiken. It had to be.

"What the hell are they doing?" she asked, shaking her head in disbelief. "If Vanessa's in there, they're going to get her killed!"

As the snowmobiles drew closer, Piper and Wade crouched behind the boulder, their eyes glued to the scene unfolding before them. The snowmobiles came to a stop just a short distance from the RV, and a group of men in black tactical gear jumped off, their weapons at the ready.

Piper recognized Aiken among them, and she felt a surge of anger. *He just wants the credit, and he doesn't care if he has to endanger Vanessa to get it. Some "family friend."*

She watched as the men surrounded the vehicle, their weapons trained on the door.

"Come on out!" Aiken shouted. "You're surrounded!"

A long, tense moment followed, the silence broken only by the sound of the idling snowmobiles.

Suddenly, the door of the RV flew open and out stepped a small family of four. The mother and father were in their forties, and their two children looked to be around ten and twelve. They all wore surprised expressions as Aiken and his men surrounded them, aiming their weapons.

This was more than Piper could take. "Enough!" she said, moving around the boulder and approaching the RV. One of Aiken's men turned his weapon on her, and Wade raised his own sidearm in response.

"I'd put that down if I were you," Wade said, his voice low and dangerous. For a moment, nobody moved. Then Aiken waved a hand at his man.

"Lower your damn weapon, would you?" he said. "Shit, we had bad intelligence." He holstered his own gun and stepped away, letting out a frustrated sigh as he grabbed his radio.

"Could someone please explain what's going on?" said the man who had stepped out of the camper. The four of them were huddled together, arms around one another. They were wearing winter jackets, but it was clear they hadn't had the time to layer up properly, and they shivered like leaves in the wind.

"We were supposed to head home earlier today," the woman said, her eyes pleading for understanding, "but we couldn't make it back up the slope. We haven't done anything wrong."

"No, you haven't," Piper said, casting her partner a weary, frustrated glance. "This has all been a huge misunderstanding, and we're very sorry for bothering you."

"Need help getting out of here?" Wade asked. "I can call someone."

"That would be nice," the woman said, crossing her arms as she shot her husband an annoyed glance. "I think I've had enough camping for a good while."

As the four campers climbed back into their RV, Piper took a closer look at the vehicle. It was actually beige, not yellow, and a far newer model than the one they were searching for.

Her heart sank. After all that effort, they had succeeded in doing nothing except terrifying four innocent campers, two of them children. Meanwhile, the real RV was out there somewhere, just waiting to be discovered.

The question was, would there still be a trail to follow when they found it? And was Vanessa even still alive?

CHAPTER NINE

Here we go again, Piper thought as the tires spun futilely, kicking up snow.

Wade, his face red as he strained against the hood of the SUV, let out a muffled grunt. "Are you in reverse?" he asked.

"Of course I'm in reverse!" Piper answered through the window, which was down just about an inch from the top. "Do you think I've never gotten stuck in the snow before?"

Several hours had passed since coming across the beige RV, the one that had held four innocent campers rather than a serial killer and his prospective victim. Since then, Piper and Wade had returned to their sector and continued to scour roads, trails, and parking lots for the yellow RV, but to no avail. This was the third time they'd gotten stuck in the snow, and it was clear from Wade's tone that his nerves were as frayed as Piper's.

"Just give it a little gas," Wade said. "Not much, or it'll just bury the tires deeper."

"I know that already," Piper snapped, feeling frustrated and exhausted. She gave the accelerator a slight nudge, and the SUV jolted backward a few inches before getting stuck again.

Straightening, Wade let out a sigh and wiped the sweat from his forehead. "Maybe we should just call it a night," he suggested. "We can have someone pick us up."

"We're almost there, Wade. Don't give up on me now."

"We've been at this for hours, Pip, and what do we have to show for it? Moving a few feet toward the road?"

Piper understood his frustration. Still, she didn't like quitting. It wasn't in her nature.

"We're almost there," she said. "We just have to keep at it."

Wade gave her a long, assessing look before shaking his head, resigned. "Fine, but we need to come up with a new approach. My back's killing me."

Piper frowned, thinking. She studied the trees along the edge of the trail. Opening her door, she stepped out and made her way toward a grove of pine saplings.

"What are you doing?" Wade asked.

"Gathering branches," she said. "We can lay them under the tires, help give them traction."

"You sure that'll work?"

"If it doesn't, we can call for help. How's that?"

After hesitating a few moments longer, Wade joined her. Together they gathered as many green branches as they could find, laying them behind the SUV's tires. Once she was satisfied with the placement, Piper climbed back into the driver's seat while Wade pushed from the front again.

The tires caught on the branches and dug in, and for a moment, the SUV didn't move. Piper shifted into reverse, giving the accelerator a little gas. The tires caught on the branches, and the SUV rolled back a few feet before getting stuck once again.

"We're making progress," Wade said, his voice strained. "I guess that's something."

"We're almost there," Piper said, feeling a sense of optimism. "Let's reposition the branches and try again."

After digging the branches out of the snow and placing them behind the tires again, Piper attempted to back up once more. This time the branches held, and the SUV lurched backward, wheels spinning as it finally emerged from the snowdrift.

Laughing with relief, Piper rolled down the window and shouted to Wade, who was following her as she drifted back toward the road. "See? I told you it would work!"

Wade chuckled and shook his head. "I should never have doubted you. Mea culpa."

Piper stopped so that Wade could get back in. He let out a deep breath that caused his lips to puff out, then armed sweat from his forehead.

"So where are we searching next?" Piper asked. "Maybe I should drive—I've got a better eye for those snowdrifts."

Wade glanced at the clock, looking troubled. "Pip, it's two in the morning. Don't you think it's about time we call it a night and head to base camp?"

As much as Piper would have liked to continue the search for Vanessa and her kidnapper, she had to admit he had a point. They had been at it for hours, with little progress to show for it. They were both exhausted and needed rest.

"Okay," she said reluctantly. "But I'm not planning to sleep the morning away—there's too much work to do."

Wade shook his head, looking amused. “Same old Pip. After you take a hot shower and crawl beneath those crisp sheets, you might feel a bit different.”

The thought of returning to the hotel seemed wrong somehow. She didn’t like the idea of sleeping in a soft bed, surrounded by modern conveniences, while Vanessa was out there roughing it somewhere in the wilderness.

“Why don’t we just head to the base camp?” she asked. “It’s a lot closer, and it sounded like they were getting some trailers together. We could sleep in one of those.”

Wade gave her a long look. “Are you serious right now?”

“Listen, Wade, I know how much you enjoy a good night’s rest—”

“Damn right,” he grumbled.

“But we should get back to give a report anyway,” she continued, ignoring his interruption. “And if anyone else has learned anything, we need to know about it.”

“That’s what the radio is for.”

“You know it’s not the same.”

They both fell silent. Wade took a deep breath and let it out slowly, looking reluctant to agree with Piper.

“Okay,” he finally said, rubbing wearily at his face. “We’ll do it your way. But if you think I’m going to settle for a tent in the snow, think again. If I can see my breath when I go to bed, something’s wrong.”

Piper, tired as she was, couldn’t help smiling.

The base camp was only a few miles away, but Piper drove slowly, studying the trees on either side of the road as she pondered where Vanessa’s kidnapper might have taken her. Her mind was still running at full speed, and she wasn’t sure how well she would be able to sleep if she didn’t find a way to slow it down.

“How you holding up?” Wade asked in a low, confidential voice.

Piper shrugged, keeping her gaze on the road. “I’m okay, I guess. Just wondering how much time we have left…and if we’re already too late.”

Wade let out a long breath. “I’m worried about you, Pip.”

She glanced at him, surprised. “Worried about me?”

“You just don’t seem to know how to take a break.”

“I like to push myself. You of all people should know that, Wade.”

He frowned, staring through the windshield. “I guess sometimes I wonder whether you’re *pushing* yourself or *punishing* yourself.”

She knew he was referring to Fiona Taylor. Piper hadn't actively been thinking of her, but now that Wade had brought her to mind, she realized that she was indeed trying in some way to correct a past failure. Saving Vanessa wouldn't bring Fiona back, but it would give Piper some peace of mind, some sense of redemption.

Maybe Wade was right. Maybe she needed to take a break, to reevaluate her motives, to make sure she was doing this for the right reasons.

"What are you trying to tell me?" she asked, her voice barely above a whisper.

He let out a heavy sigh, as if he wished he hadn't brought up the subject in the first place. "I guess I'm just trying to give you permission to go easy on yourself. You don't have to prove anything to anyone—not to me, to the Bureau brass, not to anyone."

Except myself, Piper thought. Nobody else blamed her for what had happened to Fiona, but she couldn't let herself off the hook so easily. She'd been the lead investigator on the case, the person best equipped to rescue Fiona, and she'd failed. How was she supposed to live with herself if she didn't at least try to make up for that mistake?

Maybe he's right. Maybe I need to forgive myself and move on. Thinking so and doing so, however, were two very different things.

They drove in silence for a few minutes before Wade spoke up again. "You know, I never told you this, but…I'm sorry about Fiona."

Piper felt a lump form in her throat. "It wasn't your fault, Wade."

"I know that. But I should've been there for you more, should've realized what you were going through. It's just, I was so busy hunting for leads to put us back on Gray's trail, and—"

"It's okay," she said, shaking her head. "You don't have to explain. Really."

He fell silent, staring out the window. Finally, turning toward her, he said, "I just want you to know you're not alone. What you went through before, whatever you're going through now…" He trailed off, leaving the rest unsaid, and Piper was grateful for the omission. There was something special between her and Wade, something she worried they might ruin by analyzing it too much. Despite how different they were on the surface, they were nonetheless kindred souls in a sense, and Piper was glad to be around him again, even if only for this one case.

They drove in silence for a few minutes. Up ahead, Piper spotted a cluster of trailers and vehicles on a barren patch of open ground—the base camp. She slowed, wanting to get something off her chest.

"There's something I need to say," she began.

Wade looked at her. "If it's about what I said before—"

"No, it's not that. I'm talking about Aiken."

Wade waited, his eyes bright in the darkness.

"Is he always like that?" she asked. "A loose cannon? He could've gotten someone killed, jumping the gun like that."

Wade sighed. "He can be reckless, but he's the governor's righthand man. We're just lucky he's not calling the shots."

Piper shuddered at the thought. She had the distinct impression Aiken cared more about his ego than saving Vanessa.

"Besides that," Wade continued, "he's a complicated man. I've only known him a few days, but from what I've gathered, he's never been the same since his family was killed."

"What happened?"

"Burglary gone wrong. His wife and kids were at the in-laws' house, then came home to find the burglary in progress. They made the mistake of going inside the house, and the thieves…" He let out another heavy sigh. "Let's just say they decided not to leave any loose ends."

Piper's heart sank. She knew all too well the pain of losing someone close to her. "I had no idea."

"Apparently he's been a little unpredictable since then," Wade continued. "A bit of a…loose cannon, as you put it."

"I guess I can understand that," Piper said, feeling a twinge of pity for Aiken. Losing your family was a pain she wouldn't wish on anyone.

They pulled into the base camp and parked their SUV. Piper turned off the engine and sat there, thinking.

"Still," she said, "having an ax to grind only makes him more of a liability."

Wade said nothing. After a few seconds, Piper glanced at him, wondering what he was thinking. His face was guarded, drawn inward.

"What?" she asked.

"Nothing," he said quickly, opening his door. "You're right—we'll have to be careful with him." He hesitated a moment, as if deciding whether to say something more.

"Spit it out, Wade. What's really on your mind?"

He stared through the windshield, looking worried. "I guess I'm just wondering if he's the only liability we have to deal with."

Piper's heart sank like a stone. She watched him get out, but she remained where she was a few seconds longer, wondering if her partner was beginning to regret inviting her along.

CHAPTER TEN

This can't be happening, Vanessa thought. *This must be some terrible nightmare. Nothing more.*

It was dark in the back of the RV, a darkness as thick as if she had been submerged in ink. It was cold, too, and Vanessa shivered, wrapping her jacket tightly around her body and wishing she had dressed more warmly.

She hadn't known, however, that she would be kidnapped yesterday, forced into an RV by a bearded man she had tried to help. He'd been changing his tire, looking helpless and clumsy, and she had offered to give him a hand—even turned her back on him as she did so. Now she understood it had all been a ruse, a trick to lure her away from the school.

You're too trusting, she told herself. But she couldn't help it. She had always been a kind soul, always eager to lend a hand to anyone in need. She couldn't live her life in fear, continually doubting the motives of the people around her. Most people were good, she thought, eager to do the right thing and to help those in need.

Even if that were true, however, which no longer seemed quite so certain, there were a few bad apples in every bushel, as her father liked to say. And this bearded fellow was one of them.

She had tried to fight back, of course, but the bearded man had overpowered her easily, locking her in the back of the RV and driving off into the night. There, she had been left alone with her thoughts, her fear, and the creeping sensation that she might never see her family again.

She had no idea how much time had passed since then. Hours? Days? She had lost track of time, lost track of everything except the steady thump of her heart and the occasional sounds of the outside world filtering in through the walls of the RV. Her throat was parched, her stomach empty, her bladder full to bursting, but none of these discomforts compared to the fear that spread across her mind like mold, slowly consuming her.

When would the door open again? And what would happen when it did?

A cramp started up in her leg, and she tried to shift, but her arms and legs were bound tightly behind her back, the rope digging into her skin. She began to cry, sobbing as she called out for her mother, her father, anyone who could help her.

At the thought of her father, something clicked in her mind. *Of course.* He's *the reason I've been kidnapped. He's the governor, after all, so this must be some sort of blackmail—or ransom.*

She imagined her parents receiving a ransom note in the mail, the letters pieced together from numerous newspapers, demanding a large sum in exchange for Vanessa's life. Her father would pay it, she was certain. He loved her too much not to.

But what if the kidnapper didn't actually want money? What if he got the money but decided to keep her anyway, enjoying the power he held over her and her family?

The thought was unbearable. *No,* she told herself, *it won't happen. It* can't *happen.* Her unshakable sense of justice, her conviction that everything would turn out right in the end if only she did the right thing, assured her that this most terrible of possibilities would never come to fruition.

It wouldn't. It *couldn't.*

And yet…that worm of doubt remained, writhing beneath the surface of her thoughts, refusing to be ignored.

Suddenly she heard a sound—a faint rustling coming from outside the RV. Her heart leapt in her chest.

Someone's here! she thought, desperate for something on which to pin her hopes. *They found me!*

She listened. There it was again, a soft crunching sound, like footsteps on gravel.

She called out, her voice hoarse. "Hello? Can anyone hear me?"

There was no response. The footsteps grew closer until they were just outside the door, and then—silence.

Vanessa held her breath, barely daring to move. She heard a key being inserted into the lock, and then the door creaked open.

The glow of the night sky blinded her, so accustomed had she grown to the darkness. She could see a scattering of stars, as sharp and bright as diamonds, and silhouetted against them the shape of a man. He was breathing heavily through his nostrils so that he sounded almost like a bear, and for just a moment Vanessa irrationally thought he might be one (how a bear would unlock the door, however, she did not know).

Then she became aware of the muttering. She didn't catch any words, just an undercurrent of sound, sloppy syllables without edges or distinction. Even without being able to see his face, she knew immediately who it was.

"Please," she asked in a soft, whimpering voice. "Please don't hurt me. Please—"

She fell silent as something struck her elbow. It gave off a crinkling, watery sound as it hit her, and then it started rolling away.

A water bottle.

This was followed by a second missile, which landed close to her face. A bag of chips, by the sound of it.

Vanessa squirmed toward the water bottle. With her hands and feet tied behind her back, however, it was impossible to get far.

There was a sharp click. When Vanessa looked at the man, she saw he was holding a knife in his hand. She tried to roll away as he leaned toward her, but he seized her legs and dragged them to himself. She was helpless, caught like a hooked fish.

The knife began to saw at her bonds. One by one, she felt them come apart, gradually relaxing her limbs. After being tied up so long, the pain of moving her limbs was excruciating, but she gritted her teeth and focused on the sensation of freedom slowly returning to her body.

Once the man had cut her free, he leaned back, folding the knife and returning it to his pocket.

"Who are you?" Vanessa asked, her voice shaking. "Why are you doing this?"

"Drink," he said, pointing at the water. Then he stepped away, out of sight. Vanessa heard one step, then a second. That was all. She had the distinct impression he was standing guard, perhaps waiting to see whether she would try to make a run for it.

For now, however, the only thing that mattered to her was slaking her thirst and giving her stomach something to digest. She snatched up the water bottle and drank deeply, relishing the cool liquid as it slid down her parched throat. She wiped her mouth with the back of her hand, then crawled over to the bag of chips and tore it open. The salty crunch was a welcome relief from the monotony of her captivity.

She was tipping her head back, spilling the last few crumbs into her mouth, when the man reappeared. A thrill of fear went through her at the sight of him, but she tried to hide it, masking her trepidation with a weak, crumb-laden smile.

"My name is Vanessa, by the way," she said, thinking maybe he would take pity on her if only he began to see her as a person, rather than as the object of whatever base desires had led him to kidnap her.

He did not answer, however. Instead he leaned toward her, the stench of his sweat filling the back of the RV. She tried to inch away from him, but there was nowhere to go. She was trapped, powerless.

He grabbed her arm and pulled her forward—firmly, but not roughly. She crawled on her knees to the edge of the RV, then dropped to the ground, the impact of her boots on the packed snow jarring her weary legs.

They were in a small hollow whose snow-clad sides led gradually upward. It was cold, terribly cold, and Vanessa thrust her bare hands into her pockets in a feeble attempt to warm them. She was shivering already.

The man pointed to what appeared to be a rudimentary fire pit. Someone had dug a hole in the snow, then placed a number of logs around the hole, and within these a small structure of kindling. Based on the blackened ends of a few of the sticks, it appeared someone had already tried starting a fire.

The man dug a pack of matches from his pocket and handed it to Vanessa. Then, without another word, he turned around and lumbered to the RV, slipping into the driver's seat and closing the door.

Vanessa stood there, shivering and wondering what to do. Was this a test? She had to make fire, or else—what? He would come back and hurt her? Or worse, take her away again?

She took a deep breath, trying to calm the rapid beating of her heart. Despite her love of camping, she had never made a fire before—her father had always done it. It had never looked particularly difficult, however. She could figure it out.

She knelt beside the pit and began to arrange the logs in a pyramid shape, just like she had seen her father do. She opened the matchbox—and that was when she discovered there were only three matches inside.

Three strikes and you're out, she thought, and felt a peculiar urge to giggle at the absurdity of the situation she found herself in. Then the urge passed, and she realized she had better get started before her hands grew more numb than they already were.

She struck a match. Before she could lower it to the kindling, however, the wind blew it out.

You have to cup your hand around it, she told herself, picturing the way her father had protected the flame with his hand. She struck another match, this time guarding it from the wind, and managed to light one of the sticks. The fire began to spread, moving from stick to stick.

Yes! she thought, excitedly watching the flames grow. She was greedy for the warmth, needing it more than she ever had before, and she crowded over the pit like a mother hen over an egg, all but smothering it with her body.

Then, just when she was confident she had succeeded, the small structure of kindling collapsed in on itself and the flames went out, leaving only a smoking, smoldering pile of blackened sticks.

"No, no, no!" she cried, blowing at the remains of the fire. All she succeeded in doing, however, was scattering the embers about.

She sank back on her haunches, discouraged.

"Don't worry," a tired voice said. "I couldn't get it either."

Vanessa turned to see a woman sitting on a rock a short distance away. In the dimness, Vanessa hadn't noticed her before. The woman was haggard-looking, her clothes dirty and torn, her hair hidden beneath a filthy knitted cap. Her eyes were wild and feverish, and her hands twitched in her lap as she slowly rocked back and forth.

Seeing her, Vanessa had a memory of waking up in the RV shortly after being taken, and seeing a woman bound on the floor beside her while she lay on the seats. She'd completely forgotten.

"Who are you?" she asked.

"Name's Maddie," the woman, who appeared to be in her early twenties, said. "He kidnapped me a few weeks ago, and you're the first friendly face I've seen since then. Looks like we're in this together now."

Vanessa felt a wave of relief wash over her. She wasn't alone. Maybe together they could find a way out of this.

"We need to keep trying to start this fire," Vanessa said. "The cold will kill us, if he doesn't."

Maddie only shook her head, staring intently at the snow. "I can't help."

Vanessa frowned. "What do you mean? Are you injured?"

Maddie shot a furtive, fearful glance at RV. "He'll get angry," she said in a low voice Vanessa could barely hear. "If I try to help…he'll hurt me. He wants you to do it on your own, just like I did. He's testing us."

This only puzzled Vanessa further. Had the man really dragged her all the way out here into the wilderness just to test her fire-making skills?

Maddie shook her head again, her eyes darting around nervously. "I don't know what he wants. But he's not normal. He's…he's sick in the head, you know?"

Vanessa felt a chill run down her spine. She couldn't help thinking that Maddie seemed to be a bit unhinged, as well. Was that a new development, brought on by the stress of a few weeks in captivity? Would Vanessa eventually be reduced to a similar state of mind?

She took a deep breath, exhaling slowly. "We need to escape. Maybe we can make a run for it."

Maddie shook her head quickly, a look of terror entering her eyes. "I've tried that already. He's always watching, always listening. There's only one way out."

"What's that?"

Maddie leaned forward, her wild eyes drilling into Vanessa's. "We have to kill him."

No sooner had Maddie said this than the door of the RV flew open and the man climbed out. He stalked over to the two women, his face as hard as flint.

"No more talking," he said gruffly, his voice laced with menace. "Get back to the fire."

Vanessa stood up, doing her best to keep her voice steady. "I'm trying, but I might need more matches. I'm on my last one."

He stepped closer to her, his breath hot on her face. "Then you'd better make it count," he growled, before turning on his heel and disappearing into the RV once more.

Vanessa's heart raced as she watched him go. She felt a cold sweat break out on her forehead, despite the frigid air around her. What was he planning to do? Would he hurt her if she failed the test?

She turned to Maddie, whose face had grown blank, like that of a traumatized child.

"We have to get out of here, Maddie," Vanessa whispered. "We have to try."

Maddie, however, just looked away, unwilling to even acknowledge her words.

Vanessa saw no choice but to use her final match to try to light the fire.

"Here goes nothing," she muttered, pinching the stick between her thumb and middle finger as she struck it.

The head of the match burst into flame, and she cupped her hand around it as she had done before. Then she lowered the match to the kindling, lighting one stick after the other, careful to spread the fire around as much as possible. As the kindling caught, she began to move sticks around, building a small structure so that the fire could continue to grow.

It was only when the flames were roaring and casting light into the darkness that she realized how much she had been holding her breath. Relief flooded through her, warm as the heat of the fire, and she sighed as she sank back onto her haunches, staring into the flickering orange flames.

Maddie, sensing the victory, crept over to her side, her eyes fixed on the fire. For a few moments, they sat there together, watching the flames dance and listening to the crackle of the wood.

Then, with a suddenness that made Vanessa jump, a shadow loomed behind her, and a hand reached out to grab her shoulder.

"About time," the man said, his voice low and rough. "Now come with me."

Vanessa stiffened, her heart racing as she tried to twist free of his grasp. But he was too strong, his grip like a vise.

Just when she thought she was at her kidnapper's mercy, however, Maddie scrambled to her feet and launched herself at the man, screaming as she hit him with all her might.

For a moment he seemed taken aback, his grip momentarily loosening on Vanessa's shoulder. But then he regained his balance and shoved Maddie away with brutal force. She stumbled, landing on her back with a thud, her head hitting a rock.

"No!" Vanessa cried. She tried to go to Maddie, but the bearded man yanked her back.

"Leave her," he snarled. "She's useless."

Vanessa struggled against him, but he dragged her along with him, his fingers digging into her arm painfully.

"Where are you taking me?" she demanded, fear making her voice shake.

He said nothing, but there was a hungry glint in his eye that made Vanessa's blood run cold, and she realized with a sickening feeling that they were heading toward the back of the RV.

The man flung open the door and shoved her inside. She raced back toward him, but he slammed the door in her face.

"Maddie!" she cried. "Can you hear me, Maddie?"

Her eyes flew around the cramped space, looking for any means of escape. But there was none. The RV was like a prison, a tiny, enclosed space with no windows and no way out.

She beat against the door, terrified of what was about to happen to her. Where was he taking her now? And what was going to happen to Maddie?

While she was still banging on the door, she heard the muffled sound of Maddie's voice, pleading with their captor to let her go. He didn't answer her.

"What's happening out there?" Vanessa cried, feeling helpless in a way she never had before. "What's going on?"

No answer came to her—nothing but Maddie's frantic protests, rising to a piercing scream. Unable to bear the sound any longer, Vanessa covered her ears and closed her eyes, as if by doing so she could stop what was happening to Maddie.

How long, she wondered, would it be before whatever was happening to Maddie happened to *her*?

CHAPTER ELEVEN

The first thing Piper noticed about Governor Johnston was how fragile he looked, like a broken vase whose shards had been hastily glued back together. One piece of bad news, Piper sensed, might cause him to crumble, though she had a feeling he was more likely to fly into a rage than melt into a puddle of tears.

"Care to explain what happened out there?" he asked, his gaze hard as Piper and Wade entered the tent. Piper had hoped the governor was simply looking for an update on the situation, but it was beginning to look more like an ambush.

Wade cleared his throat, looking around at the several members of Johnston's staff who were gathered in the tent. "We encountered some complications, sir. We thought it might be the kidnapper's RV, but it appears we were wrong."

"Wrong," Johnston repeated, barely holding his anger in check. "You mean because it was a different color than the one we're looking for, or because there were four innocent campers inside, two of them children?"

Wade winced at this. He looked to be at a loss for words.

"Do you have any idea what my daughter could be going through right now?" Johnston asked, his voice rising. "She's out there, scared and alone, and you're wasting time chasing after innocent people."

Piper stepped forward, trying to defuse the situation. "Governor, we understand your frustration, but we're doing everything in our power to find Vanessa. We're following every lead, and we won't stop until we bring her home."

The governor turned his glare on her. "Everything in your power? Is that what you were doing tonight, wasting all of our time focusing on that RV?"

"With all due respect, sir, if Aiken hadn't come in, guns blazing—"

"Don't you dare pin this on Aiken!" the governor roared, silencing Piper. "He was pursuing the lead you and Agent Wade found, so don't try to shift the blame onto him."

Piper bit her tongue, feeling the anger and frustration bubbling up inside of her. She couldn't believe the governor was berating them like this, not when they were doing everything they could to find his daughter.

"We understand this is very difficult for you, sir," Wade said, trying to calm the situation. "But I promise we're doing our best."

"Your best?" Johnston interrupted, his voice cold. "If tonight was your best work, then maybe I've put my daughter's life in the wrong hands."

The words hung in the air, full of menace. Wade looked startled by the implied threat. Piper, however, felt like a cornered animal. She was exhausted, discouraged, and in no mood to be blamed for someone else's mistakes.

"With all due respect, Governor Johnston," she said, "if you want us to find Vanessa, maybe you should stop yelling at us and let us do our job. I understand Aiken's a personal friend, but if Vanessa had been in that RV, there's a good chance Aiken's actions would've gotten her killed."

A stunned silence filled the tent. Piper could feel the eyes of everyone in the room on her, but she refused to back down. She was tired of being talked down to and blamed for things that were out of her control.

Johnston's face turned red with anger. "I'll deal with Aiken," he said in a low, tight voice. "I'm talking to the two of *you* right now. Aiken isn't the one who wasted our time, calling in that RV—that was you and Agent Wade."

Piper started to protest, but the governor cut her off.

"I've put a lot of trust in you, giving you as much leeway as I have," he continued, raising his voice above her objection. "I might not be personally leading this investigation, but I think you have some idea of the influence I hold, so if I decide you're off this case, you'll be off this case."

Piper said nothing, dreading what might come next.

"If you find my daughter," the governor went on, "you'll have my eternal gratitude. But if anything happens to her, if this all goes to shit…" He paused, his face hardening. "I'm holding you personally responsible."

* * *

A heavy weight bore down on Piper's shoulders as she approached the heated trailer in which a number of the members of the task force were sleeping. It was unfair, the pressure the governor was putting on her personally to find his daughter, but she had little room to complain. She had spoken up, pointing to her own skills as a tracker, and it made sense that Governor Johnston would expect her to come through, even if it was unfair for him to credit all the success or failure to one member of the group.

Wade, walking side-by-side with her through the snow, seemed to read her thoughts. "He didn't mean it, you know," he said. "About holding you personally responsible. He was just angry."

Piper said nothing. After a few more paces, Wade stepped in front of her, his face gray in the moonlight.

"I mean it," he said. "You beat yourself up enough already. I need to know that if things go sideways, I'm not going to have to worry about you."

Piper knew he was talking about Fiona. She would have liked to promise him she wouldn't take it to heart if she failed Vanessa, but she knew such a promise would be empty.

"What did you mean before?" she asked. "About me being a liability?"

His face froze. "I shouldn't have said that."

"But you did. And I think you meant it."

A few moments passed in silence.

"Do you regret coming to Alaska to find me?" she asked.

He shook his head, his eyes imploring. "No, Pip. You're the best person for the job—I still believe that. It's not that I think you're going to compromise the investigation."

"Then what is it?"

"I just don't want you to be devastated if things go sideways."

She stared at him, feeling her defenses collapsing around her. "Then let's make sure this doesn't go sideways."

He nodded, looking relieved that she wasn't angry with him, and they continued on to the trailer. He opened the door and gestured for Piper to enter.

When she heard the snores of one of the sleeping agents, however, she hesitated.

"What's wrong?" Wade asked, lowering his voice so as to avoid waking anyone.

Having spent the last year sleeping alone in her cabin deep in the remote Alaska wilderness, the thought of sharing such a small space with several men and women she didn't know made her uneasy.

"I think I'll sleep outside," she said, stepping back.

"Outside?" Wade asked, baffled. "Do you realize how cold it is?"

"I've got a polar sleeping bag. I'll be fine."

For a moment, Wade looked like he wanted to argue. Then he shrugged. "Suit yourself. But you're welcome to come inside if you get cold."

Piper smiled gratefully. "Thanks, Wade. I'll keep that in mind."

She stepped outside, the cold biting at her exposed skin. She wrapped her arms tightly around her body as she returned to the SUV, grateful for the warmth of her parka.

Retrieving the sleeping bag from the trunk of the SUV, she looked around for a place to spread it out. Then, deciding she didn't want to sleep in the open where someone might stumble across her in the dark, she lowered the rear row of seats in the vehicle and spread her bag across them.

Stripping down to her thermal underwear, she crawled inside the warm cocoon of her sleeping bag, snug and warm even as the outside temperature dropped below zero.

As she lay there in the dark, listening to the wind howling outside, she couldn't help but think about Vanessa. She imagined the young girl, scared and alone in the wilderness, and it made her heart ache. The pressure to rescue the girl, to succeed where she had failed Fiona, was almost suffocating.

Before long, she found herself drifting off into a dream. She was at the house of Professor Benjamin Graham, knocking on the door as a torrent of rain fell around her. It was night, and she only had her FBI windbreaker for warmth, so she was shivering in the cold autumn air.

"Professor Graham?" she called, glancing at the windows, which were dark. Where was he? His car was in the driveway, so why wasn't he answering the door?

She checked the time on her analog wristwatch, a gift from her father. Just past eight—a little late for a house call, certainly, but early enough that she expected him to still be awake. All she needed to do was speak with him for a few minutes, double-check some apparent contradictions in the testimony he'd given. As soon as he cleared it up, she would be out of his hair.

She knocked again, taking a breath to call his name once more. As her fist struck the door, however, the door eased open a few inches, creaking.

"Professor Graham?" Her voice was soft now, puzzled. She pushed the door the rest of the way, but it met no resistance. Nobody was there. The house was still, with no light except the occasional flash of lightning bursting through the windows.

Troubled, Piper stepped across the threshold.

The house was eerily quiet. Piper's footsteps echoed against the hardwood floor as she made her way through the dimly lit living room. The furniture was old-fashioned, with ornate patterns etched into the woodwork. It gave the room an antique feel that was both inviting and ominous. Piper couldn't shake the feeling that she wasn't alone, that someone was watching her.

She moved into the kitchen, peering into each shadowy corner as she went. The rain pounded against the windows, muffling any sound she might have heard. She was about to give up and leave when she saw a flicker of movement in the corner of her eye. She turned quickly, her hand reaching for her gun, but it was just a gust of wind rattling the shutters.

Piper let out a breath she hadn't realized she was holding.

Where is he? she wondered, suddenly feeling as if she was trespassing, violating what someone else considered a sacred space.

I shouldn't be here. I'll just call him in the morning, and we can set up a time to meet. I'm sure he'll clear everything up.

On her way back, however, a brilliant flash of lightning illuminated what appeared to be the professor's study. Curiosity compelled her forward, and she stepped into the room.

The air inside was musty and heavy with the scent of old books. A large desk, cluttered with numerous papers annotated in red ink, stood against the wall. At first glance, the ink looked almost like blood.

Studying the papers, which appeared to be essay assignments on the role of apex predators in various ecosystems, Piper began to sense there was a side to the professor she did not know. He had come across to her as a mild-mannered, even gentle person, but the criticisms she read on these university essays were surprisingly harsh, repeatedly using such words as "unimaginative," "derivative," and even "childish."

Was this the same professor she had interviewed in his classroom not so long ago? The same man who had shared his love for nature and the importance of preserving it, who had seemed so eager to help the FBI solve their case?

It was all so strange and unsettling.

As she sifted through the pages, she noticed a drawer in the desk was slightly ajar. She hesitated, then decided to investigate. She pulled the drawer open and gasped when she saw what was inside.

It was a collection of photographs of young women cowering before the camera, dirty and bruised, their eyes wild with terror. How many women were in the pictures, a dozen? More?

Hardly daring to breathe, Piper examined the time signatures on the backs of the pictures. The photographs were organized chronologically, some dating back decades. Even though the pictures showed a number of different women, they all had one thing in common.

Every single picture had been taken in the same area, a poorly lit corner where two concrete walls met. There was a concrete floor as well, and nothing else. It looked like the kind of enclosure a dangerous zoo animal might be kept inside.

Thunder bellowed outside, startling Piper. She spun around, half expecting to see the professor standing there, but she was alone.

Realizing Professor Graham was not who he appeared to be, Piper hurried out of the room, retracing her steps. She was heading for the front door when she noticed a set of stairs leading down to the basement, with a door at the base of the stairs. A faint light glowed beneath the edge of the door, a sliver of light that beckoned to her. Piper felt a shiver run down her spine at the thought of what she might find down there. She knew she should hurry outside and call for backup, but she couldn't resist the urge to discover what was hiding in the darkness.

Cautiously she walked down the stairs, her hand sliding along the wall to steady herself. The basement was cold, the air damp and musty. She could feel her breath fogging up in front of her face as she descended deeper into the darkness.

And then she saw it.

There was a single cell in the corner of the basement, the walls made of wooden boards running along the floor and iron bars rising up from them to the ceiling, the kind of bars Piper had seen often enough in horse stalls, only taller. The cell was empty, with no indication anyone had ever been there except for the name scratched on the wall in shaky letters, white against the gray of the concrete.

Fiona Taylor.

Clutching the bars with both hands, Piper sank to her knees, overcome with grief. She was too late. "No," she whispered, her voice growing louder and louder. "No, no, no, no, no—"

A hand shook her awake, and she felt the dream dissolving like morning mist.

"It's just a nightmare," Wade said, his dark face hovering above her, concern etched on his features. "You're safe, Pip."

Piper struggled to calm her breathing, the memory of the dream still fresh in her mind. She closed her eyes tightly, trying to shake off the lingering feeling of unease.

"I dreamed about Fiona," she said, her voice shaky. "Of Professor Graham's house—back before we knew him as Byron Gray. I saw the cell in the basement…" That was as far as she could get before she was overcome by the memories that flooded in.

Wade took her hand and squeezed it. "It was just a dream," he said softly. "You're here now, with me. You're okay."

Piper nodded. Inwardly, however, she sensed that a part of her was still back at that house, trapped in that basement as if she and Fiona had changed places—trapped not by Professor Graham, but by her own tortured guilt.

"What if it happens again?" she asked in a thin, weak voice. "What if I fail Vanessa just like I failed Fiona, and—"

"Shh," Wade said, squeezing her hand again. "You didn't fail Fiona. It wasn't your fault."

Piper tried to believe him, but she couldn't shrug off the weight of guilt so easily. "I could have done more. I should have suspected Professor Graham sooner."

"You did everything you could," Wade said. "He hoodwinked all of us. That won't happen again, though. We're going to find Vanessa—together."

Piper took comfort in his words, grateful for his unwavering support. As much as she prided herself on her ability to depend on herself, she was not sure she could have continued this investigation without Wade by her side.

"I'm sorry," she said, wiping away the tears that had escaped down her cheeks. "I know I shouldn't let my dreams get the best of me."

"Don't apologize," Wade said. "We all have our demons to face."

Piper fell silent, unsure what to say to this. She sat up and peered out the SUV's window. The first glow of day was hovering on the horizon, ready to spill over the rim of the world and banish the night. Everything was still, frozen, waiting.

"It's good to have someone to talk to," she said, surprised by her own admission.

Wade raised his eyebrows at her, a wondering smile on his face. "That means a lot coming from a hermit like you."

She punched his shoulder playfully. "I'm serious. My dad might've been paranoid, but I miss those years I spent with him—roughing it out in the wilderness, just the two of us, hunting and trapping and navigating by the stars, chinking our shelters with moss and oiling our gear with bear grease."

Wade made a face. "Sounds like some wonderful daddy-daughter time."

She hardly heard him—her mind was lost in memory. Her father's face surfaced in her mind, the frown of concentration as he taught her how to shoot a bow and arrow, the proud smile after she had taken down her first deer. She had been so young then, so eager to please him, to prove herself to him.

She wondered what he would think of her now, of the person she had become. Would he be proud of her, or would he shake his head in disappointment at her decision to return to civilization?

"He was my rock," she said softly. "And then he was gone."

Wade's expression softened, his eyes filling with compassion. "I'm sorry, Pip. I didn't mean to take it lightly."

Piper shrugged, trying to brush off the emotions that threatened to overwhelm her. "It's okay. I should be over it by now, right?"

Wade stared at her, all hint of humor gone from his face. "Over losing your father—losing *both* your parents?" He shook his head. "You don't get over that, not ever. The sting might go away with time…but the hurt will never completely disappear, not unless you stop loving them."

That was something Piper could never do. She took a slow breath, feeling suddenly ungrounded, like a kite ripped from a child's hand by a strong wind.

"You know," Wade said, interrupting her thoughts, "you don't have to be alone anymore. You've got me, and you've got the team. We're here for you, no matter what."

Piper turned to him, surprised by the gentleness in his voice. He was looking at her seriously.

"I can't promise we'll find Vanessa," he said carefully. "But I can promise that whatever happens, we'll figure it out together. You're not alone in this."

She felt a tremor run through her, a surge of emotion she could not quite name. It was as if she was standing on the edge of a cliff, ready to jump into the unknown.

Then there was a knock at the window, and they both turned to see Robert Tenny standing there, his eyes bright with excitement.

"We've got a new lead," he said, his voice muffled by the glass. "We think we found the RV."

CHAPTER TWELVE

"This is where the smoke was spotted," Aiken said, using a red marker to draw a circle on the topographical map lying on a table in the governor's tent.

Listening to him, Piper couldn't help but feel a touch of animosity for the way he had handled things the previous night, throwing himself recklessly into the middle of their operation just so he could take the credit. He hadn't just endangered his own life, but those of the other team members as well—not to mention the lives of the innocent campers involved.

It doesn't seem to have affected him much, she thought, still unable to believe how such a reckless, short-sighted man had become the de facto head of the task force. Technically that responsibility fell to Robert Tenny, but since Tenny deferred to Governor Johnston and Governor Johnston put his trust in Aiken, that made Aiken the one calling the shots.

One of the U.S. marshals—O'Brien, Piper thought his name was—raised his hand. "And just how did we come across this intelligence again?" he asked in a thick Texan drawl.

"A drone caught sight of it about an hour ago," Aiken answered. "They were scouring the wilderness all night."

Piper, standing at the back of the tent with Wade, leaned toward her partner and whispered, "We use drones now?"

Wade nodded. "More than you think. They've come a long way in the past year."

Piper had heard of drones before, but she'd always thought they were little more than toys for nerds to fool around with. She hadn't realized they could prove so useful in tracking down suspects.

"So what do they need me for?" she asked rhetorically.

"And we have a positive ID on the RV?" Governor Johnston, seated at the head of the table, asked. He was leaning forward on his forearms, his eyes intent on Aiken. The bags beneath his eyes suggested he hadn't slept much, and there was a cup of steaming coffee at his elbow, but he didn't touch it.

Aiken took a reluctant breath and cleared his throat. "It appears to be an RV, sir."

He has no idea what it is, Piper thought, shaking her head in wonder. *We're grasping at straws.*

O'Brien spoke what she was thinking. "So we've got smoke and something that looks like an RV," he said, his voice as slow as molasses. He waited for Aiken to nod, then continued. "What makes you think this is the kidnapper's RV, not just some innocent campers enjoying the great outdoors?" He didn't refer to the previous night's incident, but it hung in the air nonetheless, an invisible presence.

Aiken bristled at the insinuation. "Because it's private property, and since the owners don't have an RV—we checked—whoever's there is trespassing. There's public land just a few miles to the south, perfectly good for wilderness camping, so why would someone go out of their way just to trespass on private property?"

He paused, glaring around the room as if daring someone to contradict him. "Everything about this smells like our kidnapper," he added. "I'm telling you, this is where we'll find Vanessa."

Piper found herself speaking up. "But we have no real evidence for that," she interjected, feeling a surge of frustration. "It's all just speculation at this point."

Aiken stared at her, looking both surprised and enraged by her boldness. "We're doing everything we can, Agent Woods. And we don't need your negativity getting in the way."

Piper clenched her jaw, feeling her own anger rising up inside her. She fought to keep her voice level and reasonable.

"I'm just saying," she said, "we need to be cautious. We don't want to barge in there, guns blazing, just because there's a slim possibility we've found the kidnapper. We've tried that already."

Aiken glared at her coldly. He seemed to be gathering his words, coiling up like a snake preparing to strike. Before he could do so, however, Governor Johnston spoke up.

"Agent Woods has a point," he said, leaning back in his chair and rubbing his temples. "We need to be smart about this. The last thing we need is a hostage situation on our hands." Even though he was careful to avoid looking at Aiken, there was an unmistakable note of censure in his voice.

Aiken, red-faced, sat down and folded his arms, staring sullenly at the map.

"Here's what we're going to do," the governor continued, his jaw set with determination. "We'll send in a small team by helicopter to investigate the area and see if they can find any signs of Vanessa or the

RV. The rest of us will stay here and coordinate the operation from the command center."

"I'll go," Piper spoke up, surprising herself with the sudden enthusiasm in her voice. "I want to be on the ground, to see what's really going on."

Aiken gave her a condescending smile. "Thank you, Agent Woods, but we'll make the personnel decisions."

"I'm not much for maps," O'Brien interrupted, "but looking at this one, it seems to me we're talking about some rugged terrain here. If this isn't the job for an Alaskan tracker, then—and pardon me for saying so—what the hell did we bring her along for?"

Silence filled the tent. Piper's heart drummed swiftly inside her chest as she wondered what would happen.

"The marshal's right," Wade said. "Agent Woods is the best tracker this Bureau has ever seen, and I think we'd do well to give her a few moments to study the map and share her expertise."

To Piper's surprise, Aiken offered no contradiction. Everyone stared at her, waiting and watching.

Feeling suddenly exposed, she moved toward the table and studied the map.

"We already know the terrain," Aiken finally said, throwing up his hands in frustration. "That's what the drone is for."

"Just give her a minute, Carl," the governor said softly, the voice of a personal friend rather than that of an employer.

Piper focused on the map, studying the lines, reading the elevation markers. "You won't be able to land a helicopter in there," she said. "It's too mountainous, too rocky. And it isn't likely you'll get far on vehicles, either."

Aiken snorted. "Then how did that RV get there, huh? Care to explain that little mystery?"

"It must've arrived before the snow," Piper replied evenly. "And now that the snow has made travel nearly impossible, it's likely stuck there."

"All the more reason to use a helicopter. We can rappel down directly on the RV, surprise the kidnapper before he knows what's happening."

Piper looked up, horrified. "And get Vanessa killed in the process? What's the first thing the kidnapper will do when he realizes there's no escape?"

"There are risks to any plan," Aiken said with a grudging shrug. "At least this would get us there quickly."

The two stared at one another, neither backing down. Governor Johnston cleared his throat.

"We don't know what the kidnapper intends to do with my daughter," he said softly. "But it seems pretty clear what'll happen if we trap him and don't give him any options. What do you think we should do, Agent Woods?"

Aiken looked startled, but Piper took this vote of confidence in stride. She traced her finger over the map, following the contour lines.

"If we want to get close, we'll have to hike in," she said. "There's a ridge about three miles west of the RV that offers good cover. We can approach from there."

Aiken scowled, looking like he was ready to contradict her, but the governor cut him off. "Well," he said, "there's no time to lose. Let's get a team ready to hike in and investigate the area." He turned to Aiken. "Carl, I'm giving Agent Woods the lead on this. I'll still be trusting you to keep me updated on the situation, but I want her in charge on the ground."

Aiken's scowl deepened, but he didn't argue this time. He simply nodded and stalked out of the tent, muttering under his breath.

Piper took a deep breath, trying to quell the thrill of excitement and fear that twisted inside her stomach. She had been trained for this, after all. Tracking, surveillance, reconnaissance—all of it was in her blood, and now she was getting the chance to demonstrate just what she was capable of.

As she stepped outside and saw the swollen clouds overhead, however, she felt a stirring of unease. If the storm picked back up, she and the rest of the team might get stranded in the wilderness, far from civilization.

And just that quickly, this rescue operation could devolve into a suicide mission.

CHAPTER THIRTEEN

Piper brought her snowmobile to a stop as she stared up at the forbidding slope, its jagged rocks peeking out from swales of snow. It looked slick and treacherous, a disaster waiting to happen.

"This is as far as we drive," she said loudly, fighting to be heard above the steady wind. "We'll have to go on foot from here."

She was joined on this expedition by eleven others, including Wade, Aiken, Tenny, and O'Brien, all of them bundled up in thick winter gear and carrying heavy packs. Piper's own pack contained a compass, a pair of binoculars, a change of clothes in case the ones she was wearing got wet, fire-making tools, emergency rations, and a number of other items.

Footsteps crunched through the snow as Wade joined her. There was frost on his eyebrows, and his eyes were grim as he stared up at the cliff.

"We're climbing up that?" he asked in a soft voice.

Piper nodded. "It's the best way. According to the map, we'd have to go miles around to find an easier climb."

Wade shook his head slowly. "I'm not sure all these guys can make it. They're professionals, sure, but some of them spend as much time in their vehicles as they do on their feet. I don't know if they'll be able to handle this."

"Then they can drop out," Piper said, sounding harsher than she had intended. "We can't move at the pace of the slowest member of the group, not when Vanessa's life is in danger."

"I know, Pip. But we need to be careful about this. We don't want anyone getting hurt."

"It's not these people I'm worried about. We don't know how much time Vanessa has, and the longer we delay because some of our people aren't in shape—"

Wade held up a hand to stop her. "I get it." He sighed. "I'll talk to them, let them know you're going to set the pace. Just remember we're not all survivalists, okay?"

Piper nodded. As she watched her partner go, she felt a pang of guilt for her sharpness. She knew how important it was to keep the team together, to keep morale up, especially on a mission like this. But her mind was focused on one thing: finding Vanessa. That was all that mattered.

The others were still gathering their gear as Piper began her ascent. She scrambled up the stony slope, kicking at the snow with her boots to see what lay beneath it. In some places there were patches of ice, in others nothing but smooth stone. Piper had the impression that if she were to fall while halfway up the slope, it would be very difficult to slow herself down.

"Watch your footing!" she called to the rest of the team as they joined her one by one. "You don't want to take a tumble here."

Wade joined her, grunting as he hurried to keep pace with her. His foot slipped, but Piper managed to reach out and keep him from falling.

"Thanks," he said, a bit sheepish. "You've got a lot of nerve, you know, bringing a city boy out here."

"I didn't choose the terrain," Piper answered. "Our kidnapper did."

Wade lowered his voice. "You think he's out here? Or are we just wasting our time again?"

Piper paused, scanning the surrounding area with a practiced eye. There was no sign of movement or disturbance, no hint of life anywhere.

But that didn't mean they were alone.

"We can't take any chances," she said. "Right now, this is our only lead."

"I've gotta say," O'Brien said, panting as he caught up with them, "I've never felt so much like a pack mule in all my life. How many miles did you say we have once we reach the top of this ridge?"

"Three," Piper answered. "And this climb is another quarter or so."

O'Brien looked back down the slope, then shook his head at the sight of how little progress they'd made. "Well," he said, as if trying to motivate himself, "I guess it's just one foot in front of the other."

He was a big man, with a large gut that served as a counterweight to his backpack, and Piper knew he was in no condition to be on this expedition. But he showed no sign of turning back now. Beneath his cheerful exterior was a look of gritty determination, and Piper had a feeling he wouldn't turn back unless he had no other choice.

No sooner had Piper thought this than she heard a cry behind her. She turned around to see Tenny on his side in the snow, clutching at his ankle.

Piper hurried down to him, kneeling beside him. "Can you stand?" she asked.

Tenny gritted his teeth and tried to push himself up. He cried out in pain, sinking back down into the snow.

"I don't think so," he said, his voice strained. "Feels like I broke it."

Piper took a deep breath, assessing the situation. They couldn't leave him here, not in this cold. And they couldn't carry him, not with the difficult terrain ahead of them.

"We'll have to splint it," she said quickly, already pulling out her medical kit. "But first, we need to get you out of this cold."

She and Wade helped Tenny to his feet, keeping his weight off his injured ankle as they guided him to the nearest shelter—a rocky overhang that would at least provide some protection from the wind. They laid him down on a bed of snow and rocks, and Piper set to work on his ankle.

Anxiety settled on Piper as she worked. Despite how familiar she was with splinting an ankle and how efficiently she got it done, every lost second felt like a painful loss to her. They couldn't afford delays or distractions. She just hoped that, moving forward, they would not have any more accidents.

After splinting Tenny's ankle as best she could, she tightened the bandage with a grimace as Tenny groaned in pain.

"Thanks," he said weakly as she finished. "I'm sorry I slowed you all down."

"Don't worry about it," Piper said, looking him in the eyes. "You did the best you could."

Tenny nodded, his eyes flickering with gratitude.

"Now what?" a voice said. It was Aiken, looking on with an expression of disgust, as if Tenny's injury were Piper's fault. "We can't just leave him here."

As much as Piper hated agreeing with him, he was right. She raised her voice, addressing the group who had gathered at the entrance to the shelter.

"Okay," she said loudly. "We're going to need a few volunteers to go back down the slope with Officer Tenny."

Two of the others, who were also state police officers, immediately stepped forward. They helped Tenny to his feet.

"We'll do what we can from HQ," Tenny said, gritting his teeth. "Go save that girl—and when you find her kidnapper, give him hell."

Piper nodded and watched the three men begin their slow descent. Then, turning her attention back to the task at hand, she resumed her climb.

"And then there were nine," Wade murmured beside her, shooting her a worried look. Piper understood what he was feeling. They'd been climbing for less than ten minutes, and already they had lost a quarter of their team. How long would the rest of them last?

They continued their ascent, moving slowly and carefully. The wind was picking up, swirling snowflakes around them and making it difficult to see. But Piper kept her focus, leading them higher and higher up the rocky incline. Fatigue built in her muscles, but she ignored it, forcing her body to keep going even though all it wanted to do was to sit down and rest for a while.

Then she heard Wade calling her name, and she turned around. He was twenty or thirty feet behind her, and he was pointing farther down the slope at two of the U.S. marshals. One of them was leaning on his knees, catching his breath, while the other sat in the snow as he dug through his backpack.

"We're dropping like flies!" Wade called. "We need to take a break!"

Piper shook her head. "There isn't time, not now! This daylight won't last!" It was still morning, but already clouds had moved in, turning the sky an ashen gray, and fat snowflakes were beginning to swirl down. The last thing they needed was to be caught on this slope by a blinding snowstorm.

To Piper's surprise, Wade didn't protest. He merely nodded and began climbing, following the prints she had left in the snow.

Staring down at the two men, Piper had the distinct impression they weren't just taking a break. They looked defeated, exhausted, outmatched. Before long, she supposed, they would convince themselves they could do more good back at HQ, or that the RV probably didn't belong to the kidnapper anyway, and they would be heading back down to the snowmobiles.

And then there were seven, she thought.

CHAPTER FOURTEEN

Piper's skin was slick with sweat as she reached the top of the ridge. She knew this was dangerous—being wet could easily be a death sentence under such conditions—but she pushed the thought aside and focused on the view from the ridge.

Pulling out her binoculars, she began to scan the terrain to the east, searching for any signs of the RV.

"Any luck?" Wade said as he caught up with her, panting like a winded bear. He unclipped his backpack and dropped it into the snow, then leaned on his knees.

"Nothing yet," she murmured. "How's the rest of the team doing?"

"Well, it looks like we've lost three more people along the way," Wade said, straightening up. "But the rest are still pushing through. They're tough, I'll give them that."

Piper sighed. Losing more people was not what she wanted to hear. But they couldn't afford to waste time worrying about it now.

Suddenly, a glint of metal caught her eye. She adjusted her binoculars and saw it was an aluminum RV parked on the edge of a frozen lake in the valley below. She adjusted the focus of her binoculars and zoomed in, her heart racing with excitement.

"There!" she exclaimed, pointing. "Do you see it?"

Wade followed her finger and squinted into the distance. "If you're talking about snow and rocks, then sure, I see plenty of them."

She passed him the binoculars, then waited patiently while he scanned the valley. After a few moments, he lowered the binoculars, a look of recognition dawning in his eyes.

"I'll be damned," he said. "There it is. But where's the smoke?"

He passed the binoculars to Piper, and she took another look. Straining her eyes, she searched the area for a campfire or any other signs of life, but the distance was too far—and the conditions too poor—for her to make out anything else.

Still, the main thing was that she'd located the RV. Now it was just a matter of getting there.

"You find it?" a breathless voice asked. Piper turned to see O'Brien laboring up the slope, looking utterly spent. He stopped beside Wade and leaned on the FBI agent, then took a long swig from his canteen.

Piper nodded. "It's down in the valley. We should be able to make it in the next few hours."

O'Brien stared off toward the valley, a thoughtful look coming over his face. "Well," he said slowly, "I'm afraid you're going to have to go on without me."

The words surprised Piper. "You're giving up?"

He grimaced and placed a hand on his chest. "I've got a heart condition, you see," he said. "Doesn't bother me most of the time, but most of the time I'm not doing anything as crazy as this." He chuckled, then grimaced again.

"Ordinarily," he continued, "I wouldn't think much of risking my life to save an innocent girl, but I promised my wife I'd listen to my body and recognize my own limits. And I can feel it now, in my chest. I'm not going to make it much farther. I'll only slow you down."

Piper looked at him with concern. "Are you sure you're okay?"

He nodded with a sad smile. "I'm sure. You go on and find that girl. Bring her home safe."

She hesitated, wanting to argue, but then she saw the determination in his eyes. He needed to do this, needed to honor his commitment to his wife, and she couldn't fault him for that.

"You're a brave man," she said. "Risking your life just by coming out here."

He shrugged good-naturedly. "What's the point in living if you can't have a little adventure?"

She smiled, admiring his fortitude.

"Best of luck to you all," the Texan said, and then lowered himself down onto a stone. "I think I'll just sit here awhile, let the old ticker slow down."

Wade turned to one of the other four, an FBI agent carrying an olive-green backpack. "Sanders," he said, "why don't you stay with him?"

O'Brien started to protest, but Wade cut him off. "We can't have you getting a heart attack out here," he said. "No need turning yourself into bear meat."

Sanders nodded and moved toward O'Brien. That left a team of five: Aiken, his two men, Piper, and Wade.

Will any of us actually make it to the RV? Piper wondered. For her part, she knew there was no way she was going to quit; nothing short of a catastrophic injury would cause her to turn back. But she was used to the wilderness, used to living every day in similarly rugged conditions, and the rest of the team was not. She couldn't fault them for struggling, but the stakes were too high to let them hinder the rescue mission.

"We need to keep moving," she said firmly, turning her attention back to the valley and the distant RV. "We're running out of daylight, and we don't know how long this storm will last."

Aiken, grim-faced, said nothing, just went on staring in the direction of the RV, as if trying to make with his mind the journey that was so arduous for his body.

They resumed their hike, descending now into the valley, Piper in the lead once again. It wasn't long before she found herself trudging through hip-deep snow, struggling to keep her footing. The wind picked up, whistling through the trees and chilling her to the bone, and the snow continued to fall heavily, obscuring her vision.

You have to keep going, she reminded herself. *If you stop now, if you show any hesitation, it'll cause the others to waver. You have to keep them moving.*

Determined to make good time, she was focused on her progress when Aiken's voice startled her. She turned around, squinting through the snow. He was pointing off to the right, toward the mouth of a cave.

"He wants to go inside," Wade said. "Wait out the storm."

Piper shook her head. "There's no telling how long the storm might last!" she called. "We can't waste our time sitting around!"

Aiken moved toward her. He looked clumsy, high-stepping through the snow. He was red-faced and clearly unhappy.

"You're the one who wanted to be careful, aren't you?" he demanded.

The words puzzled Piper. "What are you talking about?"

"I'm talking about that RV down there. We need time for surveillance, time to see what's going on before we approach. For all we know, the kidnapper's not even there right now, and we could spook him if we go charging in."

Considering how eagerly Aiken had "charged in" last time, his words surprised Piper. Then suddenly she understood: This was all just an excuse for him to take a break. He was exhausted, and he wanted to rest for a while without losing face.

Piper narrowed her eyes, studying Aiken. She knew the type: a tough-looking guy who talked a big game, but when the going got tough, he was the first to run for cover. She was done playing games with him.

"We're not here to sit around and wait," she said, her voice firm and resolute. "We're here to rescue Vanessa Johnston, and that's exactly what we're going to do. If you can't handle it, then go back. But we're not slowing down."

A sneering smile came across Aiken's face. "Listen to her," he said. "The governor put his trust in her expertise, and now it's gone to her head." He stepped forward, leaning close to Piper's face, his eyes cold.

"I don't need your expertise," he said, "and I don't need your advice. You do what you want, but I'm going to do what I think is best for my team."

With that, he turned and began walking away. Piper opened her mouth to say something, but Wade touched her shoulder. "Let him go," he said. "He's made his decision."

Piper watched as Aiken's two men fell in step behind him, all three of them heading toward the cave. "Looks like it's just the two of us now," she said softly.

"I'm game if you are."

Piper nodded, grateful for her partner's support. "Let's go find this girl."

It was a steep descent, and Piper led the way, carefully testing each step before putting her full weight on it. The snow was deep, and it was slow going. But they managed to reach the bottom without incident.

As they trudged forward, the snow blowing into their faces, Wade called Piper's name.

"I don't know if I can do this!" he said, breathing heavily. "My legs are about to give out!"

She turned to face him. It was one thing to lose the other members of the team, but she needed Wade. She had to find some way to encourage him.

"It's not that much farther," she said. "The worst is already behind you, Wade. You've got this."

He shook his head, his eyes closed as he sucked in lungfuls of air. "It's too much. I'm tapped out, Pip—you're gonna have to do this on your own."

Hearing the defeat in his voice, it became apparent to Piper that he would need more than a few encouraging words. When Wade lost focus, only one thing got his attention: a firm kick in the pants.

She turned so that she was fully facing him. "I don't know who you are or what you've done with the Lawrence Wade I know," she said, "but I need my partner back. The Wade I know is a fighter—tough as nails. He doesn't quit, doesn't make excuses, doesn't whine because he's tired."

Wade glanced aside, looking ashamed.

"The Wade I know," she continued, "can do anything he sets his mind to, and saving an innocent life? There's no discomfort or pain he wouldn't put himself through for that, because that's just the kind of man he is."

She fell silent, watching to see what Wade would do. For a few seconds, he seemed undecided. Then he straightened, a hard gleam in his eye.

"Well, what are you staring at me for?" he asked. "We've got to get to that RV." With that, he began moving forward again, his mouth set in a grim line.

That's the Wade I know, Piper thought, falling in step beside him.

They pushed on, their determination fueling them through the biting wind and the thick snow. Piper had never been one to back down, and she wasn't about to start now. They had a job to do, and she was going to make sure they did it.

As they approached the RV, Piper peered through the snow, scanning the perimeter for any signs of movement.

The RV's curtains were drawn, making it impossible to see inside. There was no sound, no indication that anyone was in the vehicle. There were tracks in the snow, but from a distance it was impossible to tell how old they were.

She turned to Wade, who had his sidearm in his hands. He gave her a quick nod. Then, with no need for further communication, the two crept toward the RV.

As they got closer, Piper could see that the RV was old and battered, with rust spots blooming across the metal exterior. It had definitely seen better days. Despite its run-down condition, however, it was not without a certain appeal, given the fact that it was the only ready-made shelter in the vast expanse of snow-covered wilderness.

Pressing close to the side of the RV, Piper paused to listen. She heard nothing. Standing on her toes, she peered through a window, trying to see around the curtains. At first she saw nothing. Then, scanning the interior a second time, her heart seemed to stop in her chest.

There, slumped in a corner at the back of the RV, lay a young woman.

CHAPTER FIFTEEN

"Is it Vanessa?" Wade asked.

Piper shook her head, her heart still hammering. "I don't know. We have to get inside."

Wade nodded, his eyes shining with the same determination she felt. They approached the door of the RV cautiously, making sure to stay out of sight. Piper gripped her sidearm tightly, the weight of it reassuring in her hand.

When they reached the door, she turned to Wade and silently counted on her fingers.

One.

Two.

Three.

She kicked the door as hard as she could. It was an awkward gesture, given the raised height of the door, but the door was made of aluminum and it bent easily, popping open and swinging inward.

"FBI!" Wade shouted, rushing in. Piper followed on his heels, adrenaline flooding her system. It only took a few seconds, however, to discover the kidnapper was nowhere to be seen.

"Where's the girl?" Wade asked, puzzled.

Piper pointed at a paneled wall that had been erected in the middle of the RV, sectioning off the back half. "She must be on the other side of that. Maybe there's an exterior door."

Stepping back outside, they hurried around to the back of the RV and found another door. To Piper's surprise, it was unlocked. She threw it open, then stepped back, ready lest the kidnapper emerge.

The room, however, remained silent, dark, forbidding. Turning on a flashlight, Piper stepped inside.

It was, without a doubt, a prison. A few musty blankets lay on the floor, along with an empty packet of potato chips and an empty water bottle. What interested Piper far more, however, was the young woman in the corner.

She looked to be in her early twenties, dirty-haired and disheveled. Her clothes were ripped in several places, and she had bruises on her arms and face.

Dreading what she might find, Piper moved toward the woman. She stooped and touched the woman's throat, which was covered with livid bruises.

Nothing. She was dead—strangled, by the look of it.

The fact that it was not Vanessa did not offer much comfort to Piper. Whoever this young woman was, she had clearly been the victim of the same man who kidnapped Vanessa, and that made Piper feel partly responsible for her death.

Her heart sank within her. She looked back at Wade and gave a slow shake of her head. He cursed and kicked hard at the wall, causing the whole structure to shake.

Holstering her weapon, Piper sank down against the wall and lowered her face into her hands. *It's all happening again,* she thought. *I failed this girl, just like I failed Fiona.*

A tremendous weight settled on her shoulders, and she felt her resolve slipping away. She was tired of this cycle of failure and regret, tired of coming up short, tired of letting others down. This was, after all, why she'd left the Bureau a year ago.

So why had she come back? Why had she thought it would be any different this time?

"I'm so stupid," she said bitterly.

Wade stared at her, surprised. "What?"

"I should've stayed at my cabin. That's where I belong—in the wilderness, by myself, where nobody's depending on me. This is what I get for wanting to play the heroine."

Wade looked like he couldn't quite believe what he was hearing. "Are you serious?" he asked. "You want to check out on me right now, when I need you most?" He held his pointer finger and thumb an inch apart. "We were this close to catching our kidnapper, and now you want to give up?"

Piper didn't respond, didn't move. She just sat there, feeling the weight of her own failure pressing down on her. But Wade wasn't finished with her yet.

"You think you're so tough, so independent. But you're not. Nobody is. We all need someone to lean on, someone to help us when things get tough. That's what partners are for."

Piper looked up at him, surprised at the intensity of his words. "It's not about being tough," she said. "It's about failing others."

"Ah. Failing others." He nodded sarcastically. "Because your whole life has just been one big failure, is that it? Are you just going to ignore all the lives you've saved, all the killers you've brought to justice? Do they mean nothing because of a few failures?"

Piper felt a flicker of something inside her at his words—anger, maybe, or defiance. But beneath that, a seed of hope.

"They don't mean nothing," she said, her voice quieter now. "But having a positive attitude doesn't bring back the people I failed to save."

Wade's expression softened. "I'm not talking about having a positive attitude, Pip. I'm talking about being true to who you are. You don't give up on people, especially not when they need you the most. And Vanessa still needs you, now more than ever."

Piper looked up at him, tears in her eyes. "I don't know if I have it in me anymore, Wade. I don't think I can keep doing this."

Wade smiled gently at her. "You're one of the strongest people I know, Pip. You've been through hell and back, and you're still standing. You're a fighter, not a failure, and if anyone can find this girl, it's you."

Piper, flooded with grief, wasn't sure what to say to this. She felt worn out and dispirited, and as much as she wanted to believe what her partner was saying, finding Vanessa just seemed like a monumental task—not just the physical challenge of trekking through the wilderness, but the emotional and psychological challenge of battling her own demons. Did she have the energy for such a fight?

You have to try, don't you? she told herself. *Don't you owe Vanessa that much?*

"Look at what's happened," Wade continued. "We started out this rescue mission with twelve people, and now it's just the two of us—and I probably would've quit a while back, if not for you. You're the reason we're here, the reason we're closer to this killer than ever before. If you give up now, all of that effort will have been for nothing. We might as well have never come at all."

Piper looked up at him, taking in his words. He was right—she couldn't just pack up and leave now, not when they were so close to finding Vanessa. If she was going to fail Vanessa, she would rather do so while doing everything in her power to save her.

And maybe, just maybe, she would find a way to succeed.

Taking a deep breath, Piper stood up and wiped away her tears. "Okay," she said. "Let's do this for Vanessa."

Wade grinned at her, relief evident in his expression. "That's my partner," he said, clapping her on the back. "I'll radio HQ, update them on the situation so they can send someone out to extract the body."

Piper nodded and watched him head back outside. Then she crouched beside the body of the young woman.

"We'll find who did this to you," she said softly. "And he'll answer for it. I promise you that."

Piper closed the young woman's eyes. Then she stepped back outside, peering around at the wilderness that rolled for miles in every direction. The question was, where had Vanessa and her captor gone?

And how long would it be before Vanessa ended up like the young woman Piper and Wade had just found?

CHAPTER SIXTEEN

How the hell did I wind up out here? Wade thought, shivering and wrapping his arms tightly across his body.

The cold had always bothered him, ever since he was a kid. He remembered sleeping in his winter jacket as a boy because it was too expensive to turn the heat on, and since then he'd associated coldness with poverty, staying indoors as often as possible during the winter and turning the thermostat up as high as he pleased.

Now, watching Piper crouch beside the tracks in the snow, he couldn't help thinking what an odd pair the two of them made: he the summer-loving city boy, she the winter-loving country girl. Somehow, though, they seemed to find a way to bring out the best in one another.

"Given how heavily the snow is falling," Piper said, "these tracks are probably not very old—a few hours, maybe."

Wade nodded, his breath visible in the cold air. "Think we can catch up to them before nightfall?"

Piper stood up and brushed snow from her pants, a thoughtful expression on her face. "It's possible. Really depends on when they stop."

Wade nodded again and found his gaze wandering to the RV. He noticed for the first time the snow chains on the tires. Clearly the killer had come prepared for these conditions, which suggested he was familiar with the North Dakota backcountry—far more familiar than Wade was, that was for sure.

"Let's get moving," Piper said, already heading off in the direction of the tracks. "We'll follow them as far as we can until we have to set up camp for the night."

Wade hurried after her, careful not to disturb the existing tracks. He was honestly surprised Piper was still going. Back at the RV, when they discovered the young woman's body, he'd seen the defeat in Piper's eyes and thought it was all over. But she had demonstrated to him once again that she was grittier than anyone could guess at first glance.

"What can you tell from the tracks?" he asked, curious to know what details Piper might be learning from the prints.

"Besides the fact that we're following two people?" she asked. "Well, based on the overlap, it appears Vanessa was walking in front."

"That makes sense. Our killer probably wanted to keep an eye on her, make sure she didn't run away."

"Exactly," Piper said, nodding. "But there's something else. See how deep these tracks are?" She pointed. "That means they're carrying a lot of weight."

"I thought Vanessa was supposed to be pretty thin. A buck-twenty or so."

"Not if she's carrying gear."

Wade thought about this. "She didn't have any gear when she was taken from the school. You think the killer's using her like a pack mule, making her carry everything?"

Piper was silent for a few heartbeats. "Or he just has a lot of gear to transport. Could be planning to stay out here a long time."

Wade felt a sinking sensation in his stomach. This killer wasn't just some opportunistic kidnapper—he was a man with a plan, someone who knew what he was doing and how to survive in the wilderness. He had killed before and would probably keep killing until they stopped him.

But why hasn't he killed Vanessa? he wondered. *Is she useful to him somehow, and he's just keeping her alive until that usefulness runs out?*

They walked in silence for a while, the only sounds the crunching of snow beneath their boots and the wind cutting itself on the rocks. As they followed the tracks deeper into the wilderness, the snow continued to fall, and the temperature dropped even lower. Wade's hands were numb, despite the gloves he was wearing, and he longed for the warmth of a fire or a hot shower. But he didn't complain—he knew the stakes, and he'd known what he was signing up for when he agreed to come out here.

Suddenly, Piper came to a stop.

"What is it?" Wade asked, peering quickly around, his hand stealing toward his holster.

Piper bent, reached into the snow, and pulled out a small aluminum spoon.

"Must've come loose and fallen out," Wade said.

"Maybe," Piper answered. "Or Vanessa set it here deliberately when her captor wasn't looking, leaving a trail for us to follow. It's too bad we don't have a few bloodhounds with us."

"I'd take you over a bloodhound any day," Wade said, grinning. "Easier on the eyes."

She blushed a little at this, then resumed her hike. Watching her, Wade couldn't help but admire how comfortable she looked out in the wilderness. She moved with a fluid grace that Wade would have thought impossible while trudging through several feet of snow, her eyes sharp and attentive to every detail around them. He had always been captivated by her, ever since they met on their first case together. It was her passion for justice and her unwavering determination to help those in need that had drawn him to her, and he knew that he would follow her to the ends of the earth if it meant bringing Vanessa back to safety.

As they pressed on, the snow grew deeper and the wind stronger. Wade could feel his eyelashes freezing together, and he had to blink repeatedly to clear his vision. He wondered how much longer they could keep this up before they lost the trail altogether.

Just then, Piper stopped again, this time pointing to a nearby outcropping of rocks. "Look," she said, her voice so soft that he could barely hear her. "There's a cave up there."

Wade squinted, trying to make out what she was seeing. Sure enough, there was a small cave opening, just big enough for a person to crawl inside. At the sight of it, a chill ran up his spine.

Unclipping his holster, he drew his sidearm. Piper did the same, and together they made their way up the slope, drifting like two ghosts among the boulders.

They reached the cave, pausing on either side of the entrance. Wade turned on his flashlight, holding it in his left hand while he kept the pistol in his right. Then, nodding at Piper, he spun and aimed the flashlight into the cave.

His heart sank. There was nobody inside. There were, however, signs that Vanessa and her kidnapper had been there: a fire pit with charred logs, a few empty cans of food.

"Looks like they've been here recently," he said, examining the fire pit. "Maybe they're still close by."

Piper nodded, her eyes scanning the cave walls. "We'll need to be extra cautious from here on out. They might know we're on their trail."

Wade agreed, his grip tightening on his gun. As they prepared to leave the cave, something caught his eye: a flash of light reflected off a shiny surface.

"Wait," he said, holding up a hand. Crouching, he moved deeper into the cave and picked up a bullet. He showed it to Piper.

“Think it fell out accidentally?” he asked.

She shook her head, her lips pressed firmly together. “I think Vanessa left it there to warn us. Her kidnapper is armed—and he’s not afraid to fight back.”

CHAPTER SEVENTEEN

"I hate to say it," Wade said, "but we need to regroup with the others."

Piper was still staring at the bullet, still thinking about what message Vanessa might be sending them. If Vanessa had left the bullet, at least she was in a clear enough frame of mind to think to leave a warning.

"Are you hearing me, Pip?" Wade asked. "That bullet looks like it came from a hunting rifle. What would've happened if the killer had decided to lay an ambush for us, just sit up here pointing his rifle at the trail, waiting for us to show up?"

"That's assuming he knows we're following him," Piper said, her voice distant. "We can't be sure of that."

Wade frowned. "We can't be sure of anything. But we do know that we're dealing with a psychopath who's already killed more than once. He won't hesitate to pull the trigger if he gets us in his crosshairs, and we'll do no good to Vanessa if we're dead."

Piper knew he had a point. Still, she wasn't about to slow down or turn back just because her life might be in danger.

"Weren't you the one just telling me why I shouldn't give up?" she answered. "And now you're changing your mind?"

"I'm not saying we should give up on her. I'm saying we need backup. If we screw this up, they'll be sending in a rescue party for us, too."

Piper clenched her jaw, frustrated at his stubbornness. "You can do what you like," she said, "but I'm not going to waste a single precious second waiting for the cavalry to arrive, not when it could be Vanessa's last." With that, she stepped out of the cave and began descending the slope, picking up the trail once more.

"Would you just wait a minute?" Wade called, hurrying to catch up with her. "Sometimes I think you have a death wish."

"Quite the opposite, actually," she said, keeping her focus on the prints in the snow. "I'm trying to save a life. Besides, there are two of us. If he ambushes us, he'll only have the element of surprise long enough for one shot."

"Gee, that's comforting," Wade muttered. "At least one of us has a chance of surviving."

"Isn't that what it means to be a hero?" she said, trying to appeal to his nobility. "Putting your life on the line for someone else?"

Wade fell silent, grimly trudging along. It was clear he was unhappy, both with the risks they were running and with the conditions themselves, but Piper couldn't turn aside now just to put his concerns at ease. They were too close to lose valuable ground by letting the killer increase his lead.

They continued on, following the tracks deeper into the wilderness. Each step became more difficult, and Piper could feel her energy draining. Her mind kept wandering, thinking about Vanessa and what could be happening to her. She could feel the weight of the young woman's life on her shoulders, the responsibility to bring her back safe and sound.

As they made their way through a narrow defile, Piper sensed a drop in air pressure, an indication that the storm was about to get worse. Soon enough, the wind was swooping into their faces, hurtling the snow about like handfuls of sand. It took all Piper's concentration just to see the footprints in front of her.

There's one advantage to the storm, at least, she thought. *If the killer* is *waiting to ambush us, he won't be able to see far.*

The trail climbed up from the defile, and soon they were on a rocky slope. The snow was thinner here, scraped by the wind, and the tracks suddenly disappeared.

Piper stopped, frowning as she studied the terrain.

"What's wrong?" Wade asked, shouting to be heard above the wind.

She pointed at the ground. "The tracks—I can't see where they went." There were no trees or other obstacles to funnel them, making it impossible to guess where Vanessa and her kidnapper had gone. The wilderness was wide open, nothing but rolling hills and craggy slopes.

"Maybe Vanessa left us a sign," Wade suggested.

"If she did, I don't see it."

Not knowing what else to do, Piper decided to continue straight, hoping to pick up the trail again. When they reached the next snowdrift, however, she could find no sign of their quarry, and she began to worry that even if they did discover the trail again, the footprints would soon be filled in by the snow.

"What are we going to do?" Wade said, hunched forward to protect his face from the wind.

Piper took a deep breath, trying to calm her nerves as she surveyed the landscape. She knew they had to act fast before the storm got even worse and erased any signs of Vanessa and her kidnapper.

"We need to split up," she said, turning to Wade. "You go left, I'll go right. We'll try to cover as much ground as possible and see if we can find any sign of them."

Wade hesitated, clearly not thrilled with the idea of separating in such treacherous conditions. "Are you sure that's a good idea? What if one of us gets lost?"

"We won't go far—thirty, forty feet at most."

She could tell he was still skeptical.

"If you have a better idea," she said, "I'm all ears."

He shook his head, waved a hand at her, and began moving away. Piper headed in the opposite direction. She felt her heart rate increase as she plunged forward, the snow crunching beneath her boots. The wind was howling now, making it hard to hear anything but the rush of air in her ears.

You're being reckless, a voice in her head warned. *Wade doesn't know the wilderness like you do, doesn't have the skills to survive out here. If you get separated, how long will he last? Are you really willing to jeopardize his life?*

Troubled by this possibility, she turned around. She could just barely make out her partner's shape, a fixed object against the swirling snow. As much as she wanted to hurry so they didn't lose Vanessa's trail, the fact was they had already lost it. No amount of hurrying would do them any good now. They needed shelter, somewhere to pause so they could get some food in their bellies and figure out what they were going to do.

It was the only way they were ever going to find Vanessa.

She began making her way back to Wade, her pace slower now. The howling wind and the biting cold seemed to suck the energy out of her. Her mind was racing, trying to come up with a plan that would keep them safe and give them the best chance of finding Vanessa. She knew they needed shelter, something that would protect them from the storm. But where could they go?

As she approached Wade, she could see him hunched over, his back to her. He seemed to be studying the ground. She wondered if he had found something.

"Wade!" she called, her voice almost lost in the howling wind.

He straightened up, turned around, and raised a hand to signal her over. She hurried toward him, her boots sinking into the snow with every step. As she got closer, she could see that he was holding something long and dark green.

"A camping shovel?" she asked, panting from the exertion of wading through the snow.

Wade nodded. "Vanessa must've dropped it for us," he said, his voice barely audible above the wind. "Maybe she realized we'd have trouble tracking her through here."

Piper peered around, searching for any other indications as to where Vanessa and her kidnapper had gone. She couldn't see any. As much as she hated stopping, she knew they had no other choice.

"We need to find shelter," she said. "Otherwise we're just going to get lost, and that won't help anybody."

"I couldn't agree more," Wade said, making no effort to hide his relief. "Problem is, I don't see any Airbnbs around."

Piper scanned the mountain slope, searching for somewhere to shelter from the wind. She spotted another cave, this one so low that they would have to crawl inside, but it was better than nothing.

"Over there," she said, pointing. "That should do for now."

They trudged toward the cave, the wind whipping their faces and making it hard to keep their footing. Piper reached the entrance first and peered inside. It was small, barely more than a hollow in the rock, but it was dry and out of the wind.

"Come on," she said, holding out a hand to help Wade inside.

He crawled in, grunting as he squeezed through the narrow entrance. Piper followed, dragging her backpack in after her.

"Here," she said, pulling out a foil packet and handing it to Wade. "Eat this. It'll keep your energy up."

He took the packet and tore it open, revealing a protein bar. He bit into it, chewing noisily.

"What about you?" he asked between bites. "Aren't you going to eat?"

She took a thermos from her backpack and opened it, inhaling the savory steam. Then she took a spoon and dug out a spoonful of beef, potato, and carrot.

"Want a bite?" she asked.

He waved a hand. "I'll be okay. Thanks anyway."

As Piper chewed, she stared out at the storm and tried to picture the map she had studied. From what she could tell, they had continued unerringly north from the RV.

"What are you thinking about?" Wade asked.

“I guess I’m wondering where our killer is taking Vanessa. He must have a cabin or some other kind of shelter out here, somewhere he feels safe.”

Wade nodded, finishing the last of the protein bar. “Yeah, but where? This is a big wilderness. He could be anywhere.”

“And if we keep heading north,” Piper said, “we’ll be crossing into Canada before long. We must be close to the border.”

Neither spoke for a few moments. Then Wade said, “You know we can’t follow them into Canada, right?”

Piper said nothing. She knew what he was getting at: Canada was outside their jurisdiction, so they had no legal right to arrest the killer there, not without permission from Canadian authorities. The thought of stopping short because of some red tape, however, was like glass in her veins.

“I’m not going to turn back just because they’ve crossed some invisible boundary,” she said.

Wade sat up, staring at her. “Pip, this isn’t some trivial matter. We could lose our jobs over this.”

“And Vanessa could lose her life!” she answered, more sharply than she had intended.

Wade held up his hands and turned his face away, clearly frustrated.

Piper leaned back against the wall of the cave and closed her eyes, letting out a deep breath. She understood where Wade was coming from, but there had to be a solution that didn’t involve sitting on their hands or simply passing the buck to someone else.

They needed a plan. Her mind was foggy, however, the exhaustion and stress catching up with her, and she couldn’t seem to think what that plan should be.

She stared out through the cave’s entrance as the storm intensified. Somewhere in that white-out was a young woman who was counting on them to rescue her.

But what if rescuing her meant her captor would go free?

CHAPTER EIGHTEEN

Vanessa tried the door for what seemed like the thousandth time, rattling it back and forth.

"Let me out!" she cried, beating her fist against the door. "Please!"

Her fist, still partially numb from their hours-long journey through the cold, throbbed with pain from striking the heavy wooden door, and she cradled it against her chest, trying not to cry.

She had done plenty of crying already, ever since her captor locked her inside this small cabin and left to do who-knew-what. It was not as bad as the RV, she had to admit. There was a small stove that kept out the worst of the cold, a cot for her to rest on, and even a drying rack above the stove for her wet socks. Had she not been kidnapped and forced here against her will, she might have even enjoyed spending some time in such a rustic location.

Now, however, all she could think about was escape. She didn't know what the bearded man planned to do with her, but she knew it couldn't be good, especially not after what he'd done to the other woman. She needed to escape now, while he was gone. This might be her only chance.

She scanned the room for anything that could help her. There was a small window high up on the wall, too small for her to fit through, and a few pieces of furniture, but nothing that could be used to break the door down.

Desperate, she began to pace back and forth, trying to calm her racing thoughts. She needed to think, to come up with a plan. But every time she tried to focus, her mind kept returning to the image of the other woman, Maddie, lying lifeless in the RV.

Is that what's going to happen to me? she wondered. *Is it just a matter of time before he decides he's done with me, too?*

No, she couldn't let herself think like that. She had to focus on escape. But how? And what would happen if she got outside?

You'll freeze to death, that's what.

She knew this was a very real possibility—one glance out the window told her the storm had only grown in force since she and her captor had reached the cabin, and it showed no signs of slowing down.

But for all she knew, civilization might be right around the corner. She might find a road, or a cabin that was not occupied by a sociopath.

She had to try, didn't she?

Thinking these thoughts, she was surprised to see the door swing open and the bearded man enter, a pair of rabbits dangling from his hand like oversized earrings. They were frozen stiff.

"Brought you something to eat," he said in his gruff voice, gesturing with the rabbits. He didn't smile—Vanessa didn't think she had seen him smile a single time—and there was a blank, vacuous look in his eyes, as if he possessed no emotion at all—as if he were speaking to a brick wall rather than a person.

She looked away, chilled by his stare.

The bearded man set a pot of water on the stove. Then he laid the rabbits on the table and began to prepare them, his movements efficient and practiced. Vanessa watched him, her heart racing. This was her chance. She had to do something.

She edged closer to the door, ready to throw it open and run. But then she hesitated, her eyes darting to the man's knife. It was a large, sharp blade, and he wielded it with skill and ease. He didn't look up, didn't show any sign at all that he worried she might run away.

Why is he so confident? Does he think I'm too scared to run...or does he know I won't get anywhere?

Her mind raced as she tried to figure out the best course of action. She could make a run for it, hoping to lose him in the storm. Or she could try to reason with him, appeal to his humanity.

She took a deep breath and stepped closer to the man, keeping her voice low and steady. "Please let me go. I won't tell anyone about this. I just want to go home."

The man didn't respond, didn't even glance up from his work. Vanessa's heart sank. Had she made a mistake? Was he even capable of empathy?

But then, to her surprise, he spoke. "Why would you want to leave?" He looked up at her, and he seemed genuinely to not understand why she would want to escape.

"Because my family is out there. They must be worried sick by now."

He stared blankly at her a few seconds longer, then returned to his work.

I can't reason with this man. He might not even be capable of it.

That left only one option: running. But she needed to distract him, find some way to slow him down and give herself a head start.

She moved closer, glancing at the pan of water heating up on the stove before returning her attention to the rabbits. It sickened her, watching the ease with which he butchered the animals, but she pretended to be fascinated.

"I've never seen anyone butcher an animal before," she said.

"It's quite simple," he replied, still focused on his work.

Vanessa edged closer to the stove, her heart pounding. "Oh yeah? Where did you learn?"

"Hunger's the best teacher," he said with a shrug. "No grocery stores in the wilderness, so you learn to make do."

Vanessa nodded, her eyes fixed on the pot of water. She had to make her move now, before he finished preparing the rabbits. She reached for the pot, pretending to be interested in helping, and then she flung the simmering water at him.

He let out a roar of pain, dropping the knife and stumbling backwards. Vanessa took the opportunity to run, sprinting toward the door and bursting out into the storm, the freezing wind and snow battering her face as she struggled to find her footing.

She could hear the man give a shout from behind her as he gave chase. Her heart racing, she ran as fast as she could, her feet slipping in the snow with every step. She didn't dare look back.

Just keep running, she told herself, feeling both exhilarated and terrified at the same time, a heady cocktail. *Run like you've never run before.*

Up ahead, she could see something dark—trees, by the look of them. If she could just get to them, maybe she could hide and escape her captor's notice. Then, when she had caught her breath, she would set out again in search of help.

Just as she reached the edge of the trees, however, her leg caught something—a wire, it felt like, or perhaps fishing line—and she felt something close around her leg, causing her to stumble face-first into the snow.

She sat up, gasping and brushing snow from her eyes. Her leg appeared to be caught in a trap of some kind, the wire wound tightly against her pants.

She looked up and saw the bearded man approaching, his eyes dark, cold, and terribly angry.

"You shouldn't have done that, Vanessa," he said, his voice low and menacing as he reached down to grab her. "I had such high hopes for you."

CHAPTER NINETEEN

With every step through the blinding storm, Piper fought a growing sense that she was too late and Vanessa was already dead.

There was no evidence to back this up, no particular reason to believe this was true. The more she thought about it, though, the more apparent it became that if the killer realized how determined they were to rescue Vanessa, it would only give him more reason to kill her.

After all, he had killed the other woman they'd come across. Why should he spare Vanessa?

Stop thinking that way, she told herself. *You can't lose hope.*

Glancing over her shoulder, she watched Wade trudging along, bent forward against the wind. It occurred to her that they couldn't keep going this way, not with night approaching. Either she needed a clearer direction of where the killer had gone, or she needed to heed Wade's advice and wait for backup.

She was still pondering what to do when the storm thinned and she spotted a heap of stones on a hillside not far away. If she climbed up there, she reasoned, she might be able to get her bearings and figure out where they were.

She motioned to Wade, and together they trudged through the snow toward the hill. As they climbed, the wind died down and the snow began to taper off. At the top, Piper scanned the surrounding landscape, hoping to spot some sign of Vanessa or her captor.

"See anything?" Wade asked.

Piper shook her head, feeling defeated. "Nothing." She'd hoped to see a cabin or some other kind of shelter, something to indicate where the killer had taken Vanessa. All she saw, however, was pristine wilderness in every direction.

Then, studying the shape of a nearby mountain, she realized where they were.

"I know this place," she said softly, excitement stirring within her.

Wade stared at her. "What are you talking about?"

"One of his previous kills, Marie Sholan. He killed her not far from here. Remember the pictures of that path with the two chunks of rock sticking up on either side?"

“The Praying Hands,” Wade said, referring to the nickname he’d given the monument. “Yes, I remember them. But how does that help us now?”

“Rangers found the remains of a fire there, remember? If our killer was staying there before, what’s to prevent him from staying there again?”

Wade’s eyes widened as he caught on to Piper’s line of thinking. “You think he’s holed up there with Vanessa?”

“It’s a possibility,” Piper said, already starting to descend the hill. “And it’s our best lead right now.”

Wade followed her down the hill, his steps quickening as they picked up speed. “Let’s go, then. We don’t have a lot of daylight left.”

They raced through the snow, their feet crunching against the icy surface. As Piper hurried on, she couldn’t help recalling the pictures she’d seen of Marie’s dead body: lying on her back among the rocks without so much as a leaf to cover her, exposed as an offering to the gods. He’d strangled her, just as he’d strangled the woman they’d found in the RV.

Just like, Piper supposed, he would strangle Vanessa if they didn’t stop him.

As they crested a hill, Piper spotted the Praying Hands and crouched, gesturing for Wade to do the same. He seemed stiff, as if his aching legs were giving him grief, but he crouched nonetheless and stared down toward the two stony structures.

Piper slipped her binoculars from her backpack and peered through them, scanning the rocky outcroppings for any sign of movement. Nothing.

But as she lowered the binoculars, she caught sight of something in the snow near the base of the Praying Hands. Something dark and red.

Like blood.

Piper did not hesitate. Propelling herself to her feet, she sprinted forward, her heart in her throat, terrified she was too late. She heard Wade give a shout from behind her, but she ignored him.

Dread pooled within her at the thought of finding Vanessa’s body. She could sense this possibility hanging above her like a suspended judgment, ready to crush her.

She was relieved to discover, however, that what she’d seen was not blood but rather a red hat, a knitted cap of the kind Vanessa had been carrying when she disappeared.

“Don’t…do that…again,” Wade said, panting as he caught up with her. He swallowed hard. “You could’ve gotten yourself killed.”

Piper ignored the warning and picked up the hat, showing it to him. "She was here, Wade. And she's still leaving clues for us, still warning us."

Wade stared at the hat, puzzled. "I'm surprised her kidnapper wouldn't notice a thing like that."

"He can't keep an eye on her every single second. Vanessa is smart and resourceful, and she knows we're looking for her. She's doing everything she can to help us find her." *And risking frostbite,* she thought grimly. Vanessa's faith that someone was going to rescue her only increased Piper's need to find the girl and bring her back to safety.

Wade grunted, looking around. "But where is she now?"

Piper turned the hat in her hands, staring at it. Several long blonde hairs clung to the fabric, and suddenly Vanessa seemed real in a way she hadn't before. Without really knowing what she was doing, Piper lifted the hat to her face and sniffed it. There was a faint hint of vanilla—shampoo, maybe.

Wade slumped down against one of the two Praying Hands, his jaw clenched in a grimace. He seemed to be in pain, but he was too proud to say anything about it. Piper could only imagine the toll this journey was taking on his body, considering how much of a departure this was from his regular life.

We're both pushing ourselves too hard, she thought. *Neither of us will last much longer at this pace.*

Exhaustion and fatigue were creeping up on her, and she knew that if she wasn't careful, she might soon find that her judgment had been compromised. This could cause a host of dangers, not the least of which was the possibility of being caught in the open as darkness fell, with no shelter to help protect them from the plummeting temperatures.

Still, she wasn't ready to call it a night yet. They were too close to finding Vanessa.

You have to think like her kidnapper. He's a wilderness survivalist, just like you. What would you *do if you were out here, trying to evade capture with a young woman you'd just kidnapped?*

Piper closed her eyes and took a deep breath, feeling the cold air rush into her lungs. She had to clear her mind and focus on the task at hand. She had to think like the killer, figure out his next step, anticipate his every move.

Opening her eyes, she looked around, scanning the landscape. The Praying Hands were in front of them, casting long shadows across the snow, but otherwise their immediate surroundings were featureless, nothing but rolling snow-clad hills.

"He could be anywhere," Wade said, his voice low and strained. "We got lucky, coming across this place, but we can't trust our luck to hold. We need to make camp, Pip."

Piper, deep in her thoughts, hardly heard him. From what she remembered of the map, she was pretty sure there were no roads in any direction for at least ten or twenty miles. It was possible the kidnapper had stashed a vehicle somewhere, but it made little sense that he would trek into the wilderness just so he could drive out of it again.

No, he had a destination in mind, a safe place, and Piper didn't think it was a cave or some other temporary shelter. He was used to disappearing for months at a time, which was no easy feat in such a harsh environment. He needed to have a home base from which to conduct his attacks.

She studied the terrain again, thinking about what resources she would be looking for if she were building a cabin in this area. She would need timber, both for the structure itself and for firewood, and even more importantly she would need water. There was plenty of water now (all one had to do was melt snow), but in the warmer months the situation would be different.

"Pip," Wade said. "Talk to me."

Breathing deeply, she began studying the contours of the land, imagining what it might look like without snow. There had to be lakes out here somewhere, along with rivers or at least brooks. But where would they be?

Wade pushed himself to his feet and moved toward her. "Listen," he began, "I know you want to find this girl, and ordinarily I'd keep going till I dropped—"

At last she spotted what she was looking for: a pair of hills, their sides clad with aspen. Based on the way the trees were clustered on those hills, and how barren the surrounding area was, Piper felt certain there had to be a source of water flowing underneath.

"That's where we need to go!" she said, pointing into the distance.

Wade took a slow breath, as if he didn't even want to look. Then, with a skeptical expression, he turned and stared.

"What are you pointing at?" he asked.

"The trees clustered on those hills. There's a good chance that snow is hiding a brook, and if we follow that brook, I think it'll take us to our kidnapper's cabin."

Wade said nothing for a few seconds. He continued to frown, looking unconvinced. "Seems like a stretch," he said. "Assuming he does have a cabin, why do you think it would be there?"

“Because that’s where I’d put it,” Piper answered.

CHAPTER TWENTY

This was not going at all how Jacob Holland had planned.

As he dragged Vanessa kicking and screaming away from the edge of the woods that grew along the brook, where his snare had caught her, he kept blinking and rubbing at his eyes. His whole face stung from the panful of simmering water she'd thrown at him.

Ungrateful whelp, he thought, giving her a hard tug. Didn't she understand the gift he had offered her? Was he so repugnant to her that she preferred death to his company?

Using his free hand, he absently traced his mouth, rubbing one finger across the cleft in his lip. He'd grown his beard out as soon as he was old enough to do so, and in the two decades since then he hadn't once shaved it. Within a few months, he had gone from being a curiosity—or, worse, a spectacle—to a normal human being, able to fit into society just like anyone else.

Still, the damage had already been done by then. A childhood of being stared at and avoided, of seeing the other boys smirk at him and the girls whisper behind his back, had cured him of any desire to spend long in the society of others, especially those who were foolish enough to judge him by his appearance.

Even so, he couldn't deny how tiresome his solitude became sometimes. All the animals had their mates, so where was his? He could scarcely recall how many women he'd brought out here, hoping to find the one, but each had disappointed him as badly as the last. Vanessa's betrayal, however, was even more bitter because he'd sensed so strongly that she could not only develop the skills necessary to survive in the harsh wilderness, but might also possess a seed of kindness that could, given time, grow into genuine love for him, just as Belle's had for the Beast.

A high-pitched scream ripped across the frozen landscape, which was losing its glow as the sun steadily sank toward the horizon.

"You can scream all you want," he said. "There's nobody within a hundred miles."

"You're lying," she said in a tremulous voice. "My father will come for me."

"Your father has no idea where you are, so you might as well save your voice. He might be governor of the state, but when it comes to this wilderness, I'm king."

He said the words with no particular joy. He was tired, disappointed, still not entirely certain what he intended to do with her. He'd hoped so badly she would be different from the others, but in the end, she'd failed him just like all the rest.

Of course, if Vanessa hadn't seen the cabin or his face, he would have let her go. It wasn't as if he enjoyed killing, after all. He wasn't a sociopath. But neither was he foolish enough to think he could persuade her not to share what she'd seen.

If only I could cut those memories out of her brain, he thought. *Then there would be no cause to worry.*

To his surprise, he found himself trying to think of excuses for keeping her alive. He'd grown used to killing, and the act stirred very little emotion in him, but he felt a strange reluctance to end Vanessa's life. Deep down, he knew that he didn't want to be alone anymore. He wanted someone to share his life with, someone who would understand him and accept him for who he was, scars and all.

But was there such a person in the world? Or was he too much of a freak for that, beard or no beard? It wasn't romance he was looking for—he had very little interest in sex, and all the other elements of romance were a mystery to him. He wanted companionship, plain and simple: a friend to talk to, someone to share the chores with, an intelligent mind he could engage with thoughts and questions whenever the need arose.

And if he and this mystery woman should eventually develop romance, maybe even have children together, would that be so bad? Hadn't that been his dream, once upon a time?

"Please," Vanessa murmured between sobs, her voice barely audible above the whispering of her jacket against the snow. "Just let me go. I won't tell them anything."

Feeling a sharp pain in his back, Jake dropped her leg and stopped, rubbing at the strained muscle. That was another reason for having a companion—there would be someone to massage his back when it got sore, which was often.

Vanessa sat up, studying him with those wide, wondering eyes. "What are you going to do with me?" she asked.

"I haven't decided yet," he answered. "It depends on how cooperative you are." He said this to buy time. The safer she felt, the easier it would be to kill her when the time was right.

She nodded, tears still streaming down her face. "I'll do whatever you want." She was shaking now, her whole body vibrating like a tuning fork.

Jake stared at her, feeling both a vague sense of longing and a pitiless disregard. "Do you think I'm a monster?" he asked.

She blinked up at him, hesitating. "Of course not. You're just...different."

For a second, he almost believed her—that was how badly he wanted her words to be true. But he knew she was just saying what he wanted to hear. They always did that, promising the world before running off at the first opportunity.

You trusted her before, he thought, *and what did you get? A faceful of burning water.*

"I...I'd like to understand you," she said, choosing her words carefully. "I haven't really gotten to know you yet."

He glanced down at her, taking note of the way her hair fell in tangled waves around her face, her cheeks red from the cold. He could see why she might be attractive to someone, but such physical beauty made little impression on him. Her words, on the other hand...

"What do you want to know?" he asked. *Kill her,* the voice in his head ordered him. *You're just prolonging the inevitable. This ends with her death, one way or the other.*

"What happened to you?" she finally asked, her voice soft but steady. "Why do you hide from everyone?"

Jake was surprised by the question. No one had ever asked him that before, not even the women he had brought to his cabin over the years. They'd asked him why he was a "killer," as if he regularly set out to do such a thing, and why he took them out to the wilderness. But as far as his need to escape society, nobody had ever seemed to want to know why.

"It's safer here, on my own," he said. "I know the rules and don't have to answer to anyone. And the animals don't look at me like I'm a freak."

This seemed to puzzle Vanessa. "Who looks at you like you're a freak?"

This was becoming unsettlingly personal, and Jake wasn't sure he was ready for such a vulnerable conversation. Besides that, he was ready to get inside. The stinging pain of his face had eased a little, numbed by the cold, and now there was a persistent itching sensation in its place. Maybe escaping the bitter wind would help.

"I'll tell you inside," he said, gesturing for her to enter the cabin.

She gave him a perplexed look. Then, as if too cold to question his reasoning, she hurried forward, stumbling through the snow and pushing open the door.

Jake paused for a few moments, listening to the wintry silence of the wilderness. He wanted it to speak to him, to give him some sense of direction. Should he give Vanessa another chance? Maybe if he explained to her how he had become the person he was, maybe if she just heard him out, she would truly understand.

Or maybe he was just kidding himself.

Still troubled, he stepped into the cabin. Inside, the air was still and quiet, the only sounds the crackling of the fire in the hearth and the faint whistle of the wind outside.

Vanessa huddled in front of the fire, wrapping her arms around herself. She looked up as he entered, her eyes wide and curious.

"Make yourself at home," he said, gesturing to the small table and chairs in the corner. "I'll finish making dinner."

He was surprised at the sudden urge to play host, as though he were entertaining a guest in his own home. It was a foreign feeling, since most of the other women were weeping and begging for their lives by this point, and he welcomed the change.

As he set the strips of rabbit meat in a pan (there'd be no boiling water this time), he caught a glimpse of Vanessa in his peripheral vision. She was studying him closely, her expression a mix of apprehension and fascination. It was as though she were trying to piece together the puzzle of his life, to understand the man behind the scars and the isolation.

Jake stirred the meat, the familiar sizzle and smell filling the cabin. His heart raced at the thought of having someone to share a meal with, someone to talk to. It was a foreign feeling, one that he had long forgotten. Having Vanessa here with him, even if it was just for a little while longer, made him realize how much he had been missing.

She's playing you like a fiddle, the voice in his head warned. *She'll get you to lower your guard. Then, when you think you've finally won her over, she'll throttle you in your sleep.*

But no, Vanessa wouldn't do that, would she?

Look at your face. Look at what she's already *done to you.*

There was no denying how she had betrayed him. But she'd been scared, shut up in a cabin with a total stranger. If they got to know each other a little, though, they wouldn't be strangers anymore, would they?

He would give her one more chance, he decided, one more opportunity to accept his goodwill. If she broke his trust again, he would have no choice but to get rid of her. But if she could prove she genuinely cared to understand him, if she could demonstrate that she wasn't just saying what he wanted to hear—

Before he could finish the thought, his eyes settled on the edge of the table, searching for the knife he had left there when he hurried outside to chase after Vanessa.

The knife was gone.

Maybe she wouldn't be getting another chance, after all.

CHAPTER TWENTY ONE

"It's about time you gave us an update," Aiken said, an unmistakable note of condemnation in his voice.

Piper, holding the satellite phone a few inches from her head, winced at the man's tone. Even now, after Aiken—along with the rest of the team—had turned back, he still found a way to shift blame to Piper. He seemed to have a talent for it.

"Is the governor there?" she asked, glancing at Wade, who was hugging himself and stomping his feet in an effort to stay warm.

"You don't need to talk to the governor," Aiken said. "Whatever you need to tell him, you can tell me and I'll pass it along."

Piper clenched her jaw, frustrated by his stubbornness. Still, she had no way to bring the governor to the phone. She would just have to deal with Aiken, at least for now.

"Has anyone recovered the body at the RV yet?" she asked.

"Not yet. But we do think we've identified the young woman, based on your description. Maddie Hudson went missing from a truck stop several weeks ago—she worked at the diner, and she went out late at night with a bag of trash and never returned. She's probably the person you found."

Piper nodded to herself. She always felt a little better knowing the names of the victims of the killers she hunted. It helped make them more human, rather than just casualties.

"How's your progress?" Aiken asked.

"We're still tracking Vanessa and her kidnapper," she said. "We're a few miles north of the Praying Hands, where the killer left the body of one of his previous victims."

There was a pause. "I remember," Aiken finally said. "You're right on the edge of the Canadian border, then."

Piper closed her eyes, sensing what was coming next.

"Under no circumstances," he said, "are you to cross into Canada, do you understand? You have no jurisdiction there."

"I understand," Piper said tightly. "But we have reason to believe the kidnapper has a cabin in the area, and we need to find it."

"Even if that's true—and it sounds like a guess, at best—if you storm into Canada and perform an illegal arrest, the case will get thrown out and the kidnapper will go free. We need this thing to be airtight."

"And what if that costs Vanessa her life? Which matters more, saving her or putting her kidnapper behind bars?"

A few moments passed in silence. Piper breathed slowly, trying to calm herself.

"Stick to your side of the border and keep me updated," Aiken finally said. "If he's on the Canadian side, we'll contact the appropriate authorities and let them handle it."

"Copy that," Piper said, fighting the urge to hurl the phone across the snowy landscape. She lowered it, seeing no reason to continue the conversation.

"What did he say?" Wade asked, his eyebrows raised.

"He doesn't want us crossing into Canada," Piper said, her voice dripping with frustration. "Even if we have reason to believe the kidnapper has a cabin there."

Wade only nodded, showing no surprise. "Then let's hope your theory's right and we're as close to our target as you think we are."

Piper stared at the wooded valley below them. She had a feeling there was a brook down there at the bottom, and she hoped that if they followed it, the water would eventually lead them to the cabin.

"Come on," she said. "Let's get going. It's going to be dark soon."

As they descended toward the trees, Piper decided to pick up the pace, trying to outrace the night. As they reached the trees, she became aware of the soft babble of a brook.

She'd guessed correctly.

She felt a surge of hope as she continued forward, moving along even faster now. She loped through the trees like a wolf, ignoring the pain in her legs, willing herself forward. Wade floundered a short distance behind her, doing his best to catch up.

The wind picked up, causing the trees to sway. Without warning, Wade gave a shout. She turned to see him pointing up toward the tops of the trees, straight at a broken branch suspended directly above her.

A widowmaker.

The wind had already dislodged the branch, and even as Piper looked at it, she saw it sliding down toward her. She stared at it, unable to comprehend what was happening. Then, as the branch plummeted like a guillotine, Wade slammed into her and shouldered her aside.

She hit the snow with her hands outstretched. There was a loud crash behind her, and as she pushed herself up on her hands and twisted around, she saw the massive branch lying exactly where she had been standing.

If not for Wade, she would almost certainly have been killed.

"You saved my life," she said, nearly breathless with the realization of what had just happened. "If you hadn't done that—"

She stopped abruptly as she looked at Wade. He was lying on the ground, one leg pinned beneath the fallen branch.

The sight jolted Piper into action. She rushed toward him, dropped to her knees, and lifted the branch with all her strength. Grunting and grimacing, Wade managed to wriggle himself free.

"Are you alright?" she asked, studying his leg with concern.

"Oh, just peachy," he said through a tight, forced smile.

Piper hesitated, trying to think what to do. "How bad is it? Can you put weight on it?"

Wade raised his hand, an unspoken request for Piper to help him up. She did so. As he started to put weight on the ankle, however, he grimaced and sank back to the ground.

"It's pretty bad," he said. "You'll have to go on without me."

"Wade, you're half frozen already. I can't just leave you."

"Go on," he insisted, his voice firm. "I'll catch up when I can. I just need a breather."

Piper hesitated, sensing he was in more pain than he was letting on. As much as she hated the idea of going on without him, she knew he was right. She couldn't risk slowing down and losing precious time, not when Vanessa's life was on the line. That didn't mean she had to leave him empty-handed, though.

Taking off her backpack, she unzipped it and took out a pair of protein bars, a bag of trail mix, and a bottle of water. "Take these," she said. "You need to keep up your strength. And whatever you do, don't go to sleep."

Then, remembering the sat phone, she pulled it out and stuffed it into his backpack. "Now you can coordinate with base camp and let them know the situation," she added.

Wade grunted. "Not sure I have much to update them on other than the fact that I've become a cripple, but thanks anyway."

Piper smiled slightly, but she felt no sense of humor. Her pulse was drumming in her head, and she was hoping with all her heart that she was not making a terrible mistake. Her training, as well as her friendship with Wade, told her she should never leave her partner like this. But she also knew it might be the only way to save Vanessa.

“Thank you for saving my life,” she said to Wade, fighting back the fear surging up inside her. “I’ll be back for you, okay? I won’t leave you.”

He smiled gently into her eyes. “I know, Pip. I know.” Then he waved her away. “Now get out of here. Vanessa needs you more than I do.”

Hating leaving him, hoping he’d be alright, Piper gave him a long look before shouldering her backpack and hurrying off, following the brook deeper into the forest.

She would have to face the kidnapper on her own, just as she had with Byron Gray. Would the outcome be any different this time, or would the past simply repeat itself again?

CHAPTER TWENTY TWO

Wade can handle himself, Piper assured herself as she trudged ahead, watching the light fade from the forest by degrees. A frigid wind rose up, and she was grateful for the warmth of her parka, as well as boots and gloves that kept the icy cold out.

As she ventured deeper into the forest, however, following the course of the babbling brook, doubt began to creep in. What if Wade's injury was worse than she'd realized? What if he couldn't make it back to base camp on his own, let alone catch up with her? Would they be able to send a team to rescue him? How long would that take?

He won't last in the cold—not long, anyway. If he's stranded there for the night...

No, she couldn't let herself think like that. Wade knew the dangers, just as she did, and he would never forgive her if she prioritized his life over Vanessa's. The best thing she could do for him was to find Vanessa. Then, if he still needed help, she would go back for him.

For now, however, she had a young woman to rescue.

The sound of rushing water grew louder, and Piper's heartbeat rose to match it. She had an unshakable sense that she was close to her destination, close to the kidnapper and Vanessa, and nothing could turn her back now.

Then, as she was studying her surroundings in the failing light, she noticed several wire loops sticking up from a fallen log.

Snares, she thought, feeling both wary and excited at the sight. It was the first sign of human activity she'd seen in many miles, and it only confirmed her sense that she was close to the kidnapper's hideout.

Don't lower your guard now. He could be anywhere.

Up ahead, she could see a clearing. As she neared it, she became aware of tracks in the snow: human prints, by the look of them.

Her heart accelerated, and she drew her sidearm. Considering how much snow had fallen, the tracks had to be fresh—within an hour or two, she guessed. And since night was not far off, she also guessed the kidnapper must have a shelter nearby.

She stopped in her tracks, pondering what to do. If she continued forward, she might stumble right into a trap—rabbit snares might not be the only tools in the kidnapper's arsenal, after all. Maybe it would be better to get a vantage point and try to locate the killer's shelter before approaching.

Spotting a tall pine tree nearby, she decided to climb it and survey the area from above. She sheathed her sidearm and, after stowing her backpack at the base of the tree, she grabbed a branch and pulled herself up, slithering up the side of the tree and trying not to crack any of the dry boughs.

She had climbed countless trees as a kid, but this was different. This was a matter of life and death, and besides that, she was terribly exhausted from her journey so far. One little mistake might not only lead to her death, but it could also warn the kidnapper of her presence and perhaps precipitate Vanessa's death as well.

Branch by branch she climbed upward, grimly refusing to give in to exhaustion. Occasionally she paused to listen, her gaze scouring the ground far below her, but she neither heard nor saw any signs of other humans. If not for the tracks in the snow below, she might've believed she was entirely alone.

As she reached a height of about twenty feet, Piper stopped and took a deep breath, trying to steady her nerves. Looking around, she saw that the clearing was much larger than she'd first thought—at least seventy yards across.

In the center of the clearing was a small cabin, with smoke rising from the chimney. It was made of rough-hewn logs and looked like it had been built a hundred years ago. The roof was sagging, and the windows were covered with heavy drapes.

Piper's heart raced as she studied the cabin. This had to be where Vanessa was being kept—assuming she was still alive. There were no vehicles, no signs of life outside the cabin. All she knew was that two sets of prints led to the cabin.

Studying the snow more carefully from this vantage point, she was surprised to see that there were not two neat sets of tracks, as she had expected. It looked, rather, like someone had been dragged, obscuring the tracks of the person in front.

Piper felt a stab of fear, almost a physical pain. Had the kidnapper killed Vanessa at the edge of the woods? Was that what the tracks were telling her?

If he did, then her body's in the cabin. And either way, he's in there. He's not getting away this time.

She considered climbing down the tree and marching right up to the cabin, then kicking open the door. If Vanessa was alive, however, there was a good chance this method would result in a hostage situation, which she was keen to avoid. She needed to be smart if she wanted to save Vanessa.

While she was still pondering what to do, she caught movement in one of the windows, a rustling of the curtain. With furtive movements, she dug her binoculars from her pocket and held them to her face.

At first, she saw nothing. The curtains were still drifting lazily, but they were slowing. It appeared she had missed her opportunity.

Swallowing hard, angry with herself for not taking out the binoculars sooner, Piper went on staring at the window in the fading hope that the curtains would be disturbed again. Just when she was thinking of giving up, she saw movement in the corner of the window where the curtain did not cover—a passing figure, so brief Piper would have missed it had she blinked.

Hair. Long, golden hair. Just like Vanessa had.

For a few seconds, Piper could hardly breathe. It was no guarantee Vanessa was alive, of course, but it certainly made it seem likely.

But what was Piper supposed to do with this information? If Vanessa was alive, Piper had even more reason not to barge into the cabin. She couldn't just sit and wait for something to happen, though.

As she clung to the tree, shifting to make herself more comfortable on the branch beneath her, she recalled a piece of hunting advice her father had given her years ago: *Shooting is the easy part. The difficulty is in getting close.* The same principle, she supposed, applied here.

As the sun sank behind the horizon, she decided to wait until full dark had arrived. It would only take an hour or two. Then, when she was confident the kidnapper wouldn't glance out the window and see her, she would approach the cabin.

I just hope nothing happens to Vanessa. I'll never forgive myself if he hurts her while I'm sitting up here, watching.

As she rested her head back against the trunk of the tree, she couldn't help thinking of Fiona. Piper was alone here with the kidnapper and his victim, just as she'd been with Fiona and Gray. This time, however, she wouldn't let the man she was hunting evade her. She had grown since then, becoming more hardened by her guilt over Fiona's death, and now she was determined to bring this kidnapper to justice. She would do whatever it took to save Vanessa, even if it meant risking her own life.

The minutes ticked slowly by as Piper waited, her eyes fixed on the cabin in the distance. She couldn't hear anything except the rustling of the trees in the wind, and the occasional hoot of an owl. She wondered what Vanessa was going through at that moment, and she felt a surge of anger at the thought of the kidnapper hurting her.

Her eyelids began to grow heavy. It was a testimony to how hard she had pushed herself that her body was even tempted by the thought of sleep while crammed in a tree. But she had to stay awake, had to remain alert.

A fog descended on her mind. She would have liked to climb down to the ground and stretch her legs, but she didn't dare risk being seen.

She leaned her head back against the tree, determined to keep awake.

It seemed as if only a few seconds had passed, and suddenly she was sitting bolt upright, fully awake again. She didn't know how long she had slept, but judging by the night's darkness and the host of stars twinkling overhead, she had probably been out for a while.

Cursing her exhaustion, she began to make her descent. She moved as quietly as possible, her feet making little sound against the bark of the tree. When she reached the ground, she took a deep and calming breath.

This time it was her mother's voice, rather than her father's, that came to reassure her. She had hunted with each of them, separately and together, and she could still remember her mother's gentle, knowing voice as Piper drew her bow and took aim at a buck grazing less than thirty yards away.

You've got this. Just take it one step at a time.

Drawing her sidearm, Piper ejected the magazine and checked to make sure it was full. Then she tried to pull back the slide to load a bullet into the chamber, but the slide would not budge.

She tried a second time, more firmly this time, but the result was the same. Then, gradually, she realized the condensation within the gun must have frozen, locking the mechanism.

She slipped the gun inside her jacket, using the heat of her body to warm it. How long would it take? Ten minutes? Twenty?

An owl hooted from a nearby tree, the sound startlingly loud in the silent forest. All at once, Piper decided she had already waited too long and couldn't afford to wait even a few minutes more. There was no telling how much time, if any, Vanessa had left. Every second could be crucial.

With a deep, bracing breath, Piper began to pick her way toward the cabin. She would just have to fight the kidnapper unarmed.

CHAPTER TWENTY THREE

Piper was just about to start toward the cabin when she spotted the wolf.

It stood less than a dozen paces away, sniffing the air as it studied her, more curious than hostile. It was a majestic animal, its fur black as ink against the pale snow, and she felt a pang of awe as she watched it.

Despite the animal's intimidating size and aggressive reputation, Piper knew that wolf attacks on humans were rare, so she had little to fear from the predator. Instead, she saw it almost as a kindred soul, a lone hunter in a world of danger and opportunity. The wolf was a survivor, just like her.

For a moment, she debated whether to try to chase it off or simply wait for it to move on. But as she watched, the wolf turned away from her and began to trot off in the direction of the cabin, its nose to the ground as it followed a scent trail.

Without a second thought, Piper followed.

The wolf led her through the trees, its movements fluid and graceful as it navigated the broken snow. Piper struggled to keep up, feeling clumsy and cumbersome in comparison to the wolf. She was not superstitious, but she nevertheless couldn't help thinking of the wolf's presence as an omen, a sign that she was on the right path. She had always been drawn to animals, to their primal instincts and raw power. And in that moment, she felt a kinship with the wolf, a shared sense of purpose.

As they approached the cabin, however, the wolf suddenly stopped. It sniffed the air, then lowered its nose and sniffed the snow. Coming to a decision, it took a sharp turn and veered off, loping into the woods.

What's that supposed to mean? Piper wondered. She felt certain that her mother, an Inuit, would have interpreted the wolf's behavior as a warning of danger—she had known the wilderness and its animals like the pulse of her own heartbeat, and she had taught Piper to read many of the subtleties of animal behavior that often went unnoticed by others. In this case, it seemed as if something had spooked the wolf.

Piper, however, did not have the luxury of avoiding danger. She was not some child wandering through the forest like Hansel and Gretel. The danger was the very thing she had come to confront.

Her heart accelerated as she studied the cabin up close. She could see light coming from the windows, casting a warm glow onto the snow. She felt a rush of adrenaline as she realized that this was it, the moment she had been waiting for.

Here goes nothing.

She stepped forward…

And before she knew what was happening, she found herself face-down in the snow. Something was clutching her ankle tightly—a rope or string of some kind. She tried to pull herself free, and in response she heard a sharp, metallic rattling break the still night.

All at once, it became dreadfully clear what was going on. She had stepped into a snare, a snare connected to an alarm bell (it sounded like a tin can with rocks inside it), and now whatever sense of surprise she had worked so hard to maintain was gone.

The kidnapper had to know she was here.

As she fumbled to pull her knife from her pocket so she could cut herself free, the cabin door creaked open. She heard footsteps approaching, and she looked up to see a large, bearded man striding toward her, clutching a rifle in both hands.

Realizing she could not cut herself free in time, Piper acted on instinct and drew her sidearm. The mechanism was frozen, of course, and she could not fire the weapon, but the bearded man did not know that.

"Stop where you are!" she said, aiming at his chest. "FBI!"

He stopped in his tracks, staring at the weapon. Then, with a slow, almost owl-like twist of his neck, he made a show of peering around the clearing.

"I don't see the rest of your team," he said. "Or did you come all the way out here alone?"

"They're not far away," she answered, continuing to bluff him. "Now toss the rifle into the snow."

The bearded man made no move to comply. He simply went on staring at her, looking both curious and faintly amused.

"I don't think I believe you," he finally said.

"You have no choice," she said firmly. "If you don't toss the rifle, I'll shoot."

The bearded man raised an eyebrow, still looking amused. "Really? You'll kill me just like that?"

"If you force me to, I will."

He seemed to consider this for a moment. Then, with infinite slowness, he began to raise the rifle.

“Stop!” she shouted, tightening her finger on the trigger, hoping that perhaps she could force the mechanism to work. “Don’t do it!”

The rifle, however, continued to rise, and soon it was pointing straight at her. She pulled the trigger with all her strength, but it would not budge. It was almost as if she had left the safety on, though she was certain she hadn’t.

“Go ahead,” the bearded man said. “What are you waiting for?”

Piper felt a surge of panic. He knew she was bluffing. She had counted on the element of surprise, on the shock of the gun to keep him at bay. But now she was defenseless, trapped in a snare, at the mercy of a man who held all the cards. She had no choice but to rely on her wits.

“You don’t want to do this,” she said, trying to reason with him. “You’ll only make things worse for yourself if you harm me.”

He didn’t answer. He simply continued to stare at her, his finger tightening on the trigger.

Piper tried to think of a way out. She couldn’t cut herself free, and she couldn’t fire her gun. But there had to be something she could do.

“Why did you keep two of them?” she blurted out, expressing one of the questions she had asked herself a number of times.

His eyebrows pulled together. “Two of them?”

“Two women at the same time. You broke the pattern. In the past, you always dealt with one victim at a time, but this time you did something different. Why?”

“Victim,” he repeated, sounding disgusted by the word. “Is that what you think this is about? You think I’m just some creep victimizing women for my own gratification?”

Piper couldn’t believe what she was hearing. Was this man truly trying to defend his actions? She felt a surge of anger and disgust well up within her, but she couldn’t let it show. She had to keep him talking, keep him distracted. It was the only way to give herself a chance to escape.

“What else could it be about?” she asked, trying to sound calm and controlled. “You’re taking women against their will, locking them up in this cabin. What other explanation is there?”

The bearded man shook his head, a look of frustration on his face. “You law enforcement types are all the same. You think you know everything. But you have no idea who I am or what I’m doing, so stop pretending you have me figured out.”

“Okay,” Piper said. With an effort, as if the gun really could fire, she lowered her weapon. “So tell me. Why are you doing all this?”

For a few seconds he stared at her, looking like he was considering her words. Then he gestured with the rifle.

"Toss the gun," he said.

Piper hesitated, not wanting to give in. Then again, the gun was useless. The bearded man had to know that.

With a resigned sigh, she tossed her gun aside, watching as it landed in the snow. The bearded man lowered his own rifle, but he didn't put it down.

"The women I've brought out here weren't victims," he said, his voice low and intense. "I took them because I wanted to offer them a life they couldn't have in any other way."

"A life of isolation?"

"A life of freedom! Freedom from the pressures of society, from the expectations of others. I give them a chance to escape, to start anew."

Piper's mind raced. This man was delusional, but she had to keep him talking, keep him engaged so she could find a way out.

"And what about hurting them?" she asked, trying to sound sympathetic. "If your purpose was to give them a gift, then why'd you kill them? Is that what happens when someone refuses?"

The glassy look in his eyes made it clear he was done answering questions. He raised the rifle and aimed down the barrel at her. "Throw the knife into the snow, too," he said.

Damn it! Piper thought. *How'd he see it?*

She might've bluffed with him, but that didn't mean he was going to bluff with her. Her only hope was that he would find some reason to keep her alive, some reason not to shoot her. If she could just get him to come a little closer…

Lifting the knife from her side, she cocked her arm back and paused. "I wasn't lying when I told you my team is on their way," she said. "If you fire that rifle, they'll know exactly where we are, and they'll come down on you with a vengeance."

"So they don't know where we are, then?" he asked, a triumphant look in his eyes, and Piper realized she'd made a mistake. Now he would know he had time—time to kill her and make his escape, perhaps, rather than holing up in the cabin and waiting for reinforcements to arrive.

Gradually, he lowered the rifle. He stepped toward her, turning the rifle in his hands.

"Then I'll just have to kill you quietly," he said, and he swung the butt of the rifle at her face.

CHAPTER TWENTY FOUR

At the last moment, Piper rolled to the side, narrowly escaping the blow. There was a hard thump as the rifle struck the packed snow. Then, still restrained by the trap, Piper used her free leg to kick up at her attacker. Her shin connected with his thigh, and he staggered, lowering the rifle.

Taking advantage of his surprise, she grabbed the rifle and tried to wrestle it away from him. He was too strong, however, and she quickly realized she couldn't simply overpower him.

Still holding onto the rifle, she wrapped her legs around her attacker's and gave the weapon a hard tug. One of his feet caught on the snare's wire, and he stumbled away from her.

Picking up the knife from where she'd dropped it, she began to saw furiously at the snare. She was dimly aware of the sound of Vanessa pounding on the door of the cabin—she was alive, after all.

Piper, however, did not have long to appreciate this realization. The killer was already rising, pushing himself to his feet.

Come on, come on! she thought, willing the snare to break. In only a few seconds, she knew, the man would turn the rifle on her, and she had a feeling he wouldn't care how much noise he made so long as it got rid of her.

The man regained his footing and, breathing heavily, began to turn toward her. Just when Piper felt certain her life was over, the wire snapped and her leg came free.

She sprang to her feet. Knowing it would be suicide to rush her attacker now, she raced away from him instead, hoping the darkness would conceal her if she could just get back to the forest. She needed to lure him away from the cabin, make sure that—no matter what else happened—he didn't harm Vanessa.

A gunshot cracked the night, and a bullet punched into the snow beside Piper. She glanced back and saw the man had raised the rifle again. She knew she couldn't outrun a bullet, so she dove into a snowdrift, curling up tightly and holding her breath.

She heard the crunch of boots in the snow and the creak of the rifle as her attacker aimed it at the snowdrift. Piper closed her eyes, knowing that this could be it. It was entirely possible that she was about to die in this desolate place, far from anyone who would mourn her.

The shot rang out, and for a moment, there was silence. Then she realized the shot hadn't hit her. Hardly believing her luck, she rose and darted toward the forest like a rabbit flushed from hiding, her heart pounding in her chest. She could hear him giving chase, his steps not far behind her, but she didn't dare look back again.

The rifle cracked again as she neared the trees, and bark exploded in front of her. She ducked, stumbled, then threw herself behind a tree just as a bullet narrowly missed her.

Just lure him away, she told herself. *Someone from the team will eventually follow your tracks, find the cabin, and rescue Vanessa. It might take hours, but it'll happen. All you have to do is get the killer out of the way.*

It occurred to her that if she did manage to draw the killer away, she would also be taking herself farther and farther from any hope of rescue. That was a sacrifice she was more than willing to make, however.

Just as she was wondering how well the tree would protect her, she felt the hard impact of a bullet on the opposite side of it.

"Come on out!" the bearded man said. "I'll make it quick. Otherwise, no promises."

Fighting back a surge of panic, injecting as much confidence into her voice as she could, Piper called back, "First you'll have to catch me!"

Then she ran, zigzagging through the trees, ducking as a bullet flew overhead.

If she ventured far enough, she knew, her pursuer would eventually grow tired of the chase and return to his cabin. Vanessa was, after all, his prize. Piper was just the pesky FBI agent in his way. Even though her instincts were screaming at her to save her own skin, she couldn't let this happen.

She hadn't come out here to back down from the killer, but to lead him back to civilization in handcuffs. And that was exactly what she meant to do.

The wind was kicking up again, and with it came flurries of snow that swirled about, blinding her and obscuring what little there was to see of the forest. She knew he had to be a skilled hunter and tracker—it was the only way one could survive in such rugged conditions. That meant she could rely on him to follow her tracks.

And step right into her trap, just as she'd stepped into his.

Piper ran until her lungs burned and her legs ached, then slowed down to a jog. She had to keep moving, but she couldn't keep up the same pace forever. She was exhausted, freezing, and could feel herself losing momentum rapidly.

Just keep going, she told herself. *All you have to do is get a lead on him.*

As fatigue took its toll, however, she found herself slowing. She leaned against a tree for support, panting. Her fingers were numb from the cold, and she could feel her body trembling with exhaustion. She didn't know how much longer she could keep up like this after such a grueling day.

Looking over her shoulder, she searched the woods for signs of movement. Nothing stirred, nothing shifted. From what her eyes told her, she seemed to be entirely alone. She knew better than to rely solely on her sight, however. She sensed him nearby, lurking in the shadows, perhaps even aiming down the sights of his rifle that very moment.

Forcing herself to keep moving, she moved into a thicket where the aspens grew close together. Then, doubling back in a wide loop, she came within five or six feet of the tracks she had left only a few minutes earlier.

Still she saw no sign of her attacker.

What if he went back to the cabin? she thought, fighting a growing sense of panic. *What will he do to Vanessa?*

But she couldn't think about that now, couldn't explore all the ways this might go wrong. Instead she turned her focus on a large pine tree, similar to the one she had climbed earlier, and began to scramble up it.

Her arms ached as she hefted herself up the tree, her hands raw and pained from the cold. When she was about eight or ten feet above the trail she had left, she wedged herself in a fork in the tree and waited.

The seconds dragged by like hours. Her fear that her attacker might have turned back began to grow inside her, spreading like mold across her thoughts, poisoning her until she felt a dreadful certainty that she had failed and Vanessa was already dead.

Please, she thought, unsure whom she was addressing. *Please give me another chance. Please don't let me fail again, not like this.*

Then she saw him, drifting through the trees like a phantom, his eyes studying his surroundings with the laser-like focus of a hunter.

Piper waited with bated breath. Then, when he was almost directly beneath her, she threw herself from the tree, colliding with the man and knocking him into the snow.

The rifle went off, the sound deafening in the still forest. Then she was grappling with him, trying to pin him down. He had dropped the rifle, freeing up his hands so he could fight back, and one of his bear-like hands closed around Piper's neck.

Piper gasped for air, her eyes widening in horror as she felt the man's grip tighten. She could feel his fingers working their way up beneath her chin, pushing against the delicate tenderness of her throat and threatening to crush it. He was strong and wild now, no longer the quiet stalker but a desperate animal that had been cornered and was now fighting for its life.

Panicked, Piper thrust her arm between them, trying to create some space between them so she could draw breath. But it was too late; the man had already started to strangle her. His grip was like iron, his fingers crushing her windpipe.

Fear bloomed inside her like a bloodstain, and her thoughts raced feverishly, demanding she do something—anything—to escape the crushing weight of the man's hands. She scratched at his hands, pulled at his fingers, but nothing worked. He was simply too strong.

As the man's grip tightened around her throat, she found herself thinking back on all the lessons her father had taught her over the years: how to read maps, identify animal tracks in the snow, and, most importantly, how to keep herself under control no matter how bad the situation was.

The most challenging enemy you will ever face is yourself, he had told her. *It is easier to tame a wolf than to tame your own spirit, but if you can keep yourself under control, if you can master your own fears, there is no challenge you cannot conquer.*

As her consciousness began to ebb, growing dark at the edges, she tried to calm herself and find one moment of clarity. She had to do something to change the odds, but what? He was too powerful, and every moment she was growing weaker, losing her grip on reality. How could she—

Then she saw it: a dead branch hanging in the air just above the man's head. Forcing herself to let go of his hands, she reached up and snapped off the end of the branch. Then, before the man could react, she struck him hard across the face.

He stumbled back, crying out and covering his eyes. Free of the pressure of the man's hands, Piper gasped for air, her throat burning. She could hardly believe she was still alive. Stars danced before her eyes, and her stomach seized up, causing her to retch.

Get up! she screamed at herself. *Get up!*

Pulling herself together with a Herculean effort, she rose. The man was leaning on his hands, which were buried in the snow up to his elbows. He was panting.

"It's over," she said, pausing to cough. "I'm placing you under arrest."

He made no move, nor did he say anything. Piper took a step toward him…

In one quick movement, he rose, spinning toward her, the rifle in his hands now. He must have found it beneath the snow. Even in the dimness of the forest Piper could see his eyes blazing with rage, more animal than human now. He had been humiliated and he wanted revenge.

Looking into those mad eyes, she knew the time for talk was over. There would be no chance to reason with him, no opportunity to explain to him why it was in his best interest not to kill her.

He was going to pull that trigger, one way or the other.

Then, as the bearded man's mouth tightened into a grimace, Piper heard a gunshot and saw bark explode just to the man's left. He spun, searching the woods for the source of the gunshot, and another bullet whistled past him.

Piper wasted no time. Taking advantage of the distraction, she barreled into the bearded man and sent him sprawling into the snow. Before he could recover from this surprise, she had pinned his arms behind his back and cuffed them.

"You're under arrest," she said, her voice trembling slightly. "Don't move."

The man howled in rage, but it was too late; Piper had won the battle.

As Piper finished handcuffing him, Wade emerged from the trees nearby and limped to her side, keeping his gun trained on the bearded man to make sure there would be no more surprises.

"Are you okay?" he asked Piper, concern filling his voice.

Piper nodded tiredly. "I'm alive, and right now, I think that's all that counts."

* * *

As they trudged through the snow, Wade limping along and doing his best to keep his gun trained on the bearded man, Piper prayed they were not too late to save Vanessa.

"Is she still alive?" she asked the bearded man. Yes, she had heard Vanessa banging at the cabin door, but what if she was gravely injured, close to death?

He refused to answer. He simply kept his eyes fixed forward, his jaw clenched tight, and walked in stony silence. Piper knew there was no point in pushing him; he had made up his mind and there was nothing she could do to make him talk.

"Don't worry," Wade said. "From everything we know about her, she's a fighter. We can't give up hope."

Piper nodded, but inwardly she was struggling not to surrender to fear. The very reason she had initially refused to help with this investigation was the fear that she would experience a repeat of the Byron Gray case, and Piper was terrified she had failed to save the killer's intended victim yet again. She clung to the hope that this case, unlike the other, would have a happy ending.

"I can't believe you found me," she said to Wade, grateful for his assistance.

Wade shrugged. "All I did was follow your tracks. You were the one who charged into danger to save a stranger. That's impressive."

Piper smiled faintly and looked ahead, her eyes searching the darkness. As she focused on their mission, the fear began to fade, replaced by determination and resolve. There was no time to dwell on what had happened; they needed to press onward and rescue Vanessa before it was too late.

As they broke through the trees and spotted the cabin, she was surprised to see a band of light glowing in the east. How had the night passed so quickly? She must've slept longer than she'd realized.

"How do you want to do this?" Wade asked. "Do you want to stay with our new friend here, and I'll go?"

Piper knew what he was getting at. If Vanessa was dead in that cabin, Wade didn't want her to be the one to find the young woman's body. But Piper hadn't come all this way just to let someone else step up in her place.

"No," she said softly, steeling herself for whatever she might find. "I'll go."

She approached the cabin cautiously, her heart pounding in her chest. She was not sure if she was ready to face what was on the other side of that door. The thought of prolonging this uncertainty any longer, however, was far worse than the thought of discovering the truth.

A pair of latches, little more than blocks rotating on screws, kept the door from being opened from the inside. Piper turned these, hardly daring to breathe.

This was it, the moment she had both feared and longed for.

She pushed the door open. It swung slowly, reluctantly, with a low groan, gradually revealing a small room with hardwood furniture that appeared to have been handmade by whoever had built the cabin. The stove let out a faint ticking sound as the metal slowly shrank, suggesting no wood had been placed on it for a long time.

"Vanessa?" Piper called, her voice trembling. No answer came. Piper was just beginning to give up hope when she noticed a figure huddled on an old mattress in the corner of the room, bundled up in blankets.

Piper rushed forward, kneeling down beside the figure, whom she immediately recognized as none other than Vanessa Johnston. The young woman's face was pale, soot-stained, and tired-looking, but she was alive.

A tremendous sense of joy filled Piper as she gently brushed the young woman's hair back from her face. "You're safe," she whispered, repeating the words over and over, as much to herself as to Vanessa. "You're safe, you're safe, you're safe."

Vanessa's eyes fluttered. Suddenly she jerked away, scrambling against the wall and tucking her knees against her chest, staring at Piper with alarm.

"Who are you?" she asked.

"My name is Piper," Piper answered softly. "I'm with the FBI, and I'm here to rescue you."

Vanessa stared at Piper for a few seconds, as if unable to register what she'd just heard. Then she began to weep, her shoulders shaking.

"Shh," Piper said, leaning forward to wrap her arms around the young woman. "It's okay. Everything is going to be alright."

CHAPTER TWENTY FIVE

As the helicopter touched down at the base camp, the blades whipping the air into a maelstrom, Piper guided Vanessa to the ground and led her toward the tent. They had only gone a few paces when the tent flap was thrown back and Governor Johnston strode out, breaking into a run when he saw his daughter.

Piper stopped and let Vanessa go on ahead of her. As she watched the governor race forward and wrap his daughter in his arms, lifting her off the ground, Piper realized this was why she did what she did: for moments like this. Putting away killers was satisfying as well, but there was nothing like the feeling of reuniting a family torn apart by tragedy.

Wade joined her, casting a glance over at the emotional reunion. "Makes it all worthwhile, doesn't it?" he said.

She nodded, having no words at the moment. Johnston was still holding his daughter, and Piper could tell by the way he was shaking that he must be weeping. She averted her eyes, giving him some privacy.

"You never doubted me, did you?" she asked Wade.

"Not for a second," he said without hesitation. "I wouldn't have gone all the way to Alaska to find you if I didn't think you were the right person for the job."

Piper smiled, grateful for his unwavering support. "Thank you. I couldn't have done this without you."

Wade shrugged. "You save me, I save you. That's how it goes. We're partners, remember?"

Piper hesitated. He was speaking the way he'd spoken in the old days, before she left the Bureau. She'd told him she would only return for this one case, and she'd meant it. Did he think she had changed her mind?

He waved a hand in the air before she could ask. "I know, I know. You've got your cabin to get back to. I'm just saying…" He pursed his lips, as if trying to think of the best way to say what he meant. "We make a good team, that's all."

"We do," Piper agreed, smiling.

They both fell silent. Piper's gaze drifted back to the helicopter as the bearded man who had kidnapped Vanessa was led away by a pair of

FBI agents, his hands still cuffed behind his back and his head hanging low.

"Did we ever discover his name?" she asked Wade.

"Jacob Holland," Wade answered. "Had a troubled childhood, in and out of the foster system, eventually ending up in a juvenile detention center. He was released at eighteen but never really managed to get his life back on track. You know the story."

Piper nodded, feeling a pang of sympathy for the man they had just arrested. While his story didn't excuse his actions, it was still sad to think how his own childhood pain had led him to inflict pain on others.

"While you went into the cabin to get Vanessa," Wade said, "Holland started babbling about the 'gift' he'd given Vanessa, and how he wanted—needed—to find the right woman to be his 'mate'—which apparently meant living out in the wilderness with him."

Piper shook her head, wondering how lonely Holland must've been to resort to such methods. "Well," she said, "at least he won't be hurting anyone else now."

"No, he won't," Wade agreed.

They both fell into a comfortable silence, watching the helicopter lift off and disappear into the distance.

"So, what now?" Wade asked, breaking the quiet.

Piper turned to him, surprised by the question. She had thought this was the end of it, that she would return to her cabin and resume her solitary life.

"What do you mean?" she asked.

"I mean, what's next for you? Back to your wilderness cabin? Is that how it's going to be for the rest of your life?"

Before she could answer, she heard a voice calling her name. She turned to see Governor Johnston walking over to her, his eyes red-rimmed but filled with gratitude.

"I don't know how to thank you, Agent Woods," he said. "You saved my daughter's life. If there's anything I can ever do for you, just name it."

Piper smiled, feeling a warmth spread through her chest. "You don't owe me anything, Governor," she said. "Just seeing Vanessa reunited with her family is enough for me."

He nodded, still looking emotional. "Of course, I understand. But please, if you ever need anything, don't hesitate to ask."

"I will. Thank you, Governor."

To her surprise, the governor lingered, his eyes scanning the area. "And where is the man who did this?" he asked. "Is he being brought to justice?"

Piper nodded, gesturing toward the FBI agents leading Holland away. "He will face the full consequences of his actions."

Johnston's face hardened with determination. "Good. I want to make sure he never hurts anyone else ever again."

Piper watched him go, feeling a twinge of sympathy for the father who had nearly lost his daughter. She knew all too well the pain of loss, the feeling of helplessness when someone you loved was taken from you. But she also knew that sometimes, the only way to move forward was to let go of the past and embrace the present.

Wade was checking his watch. "We should get going. We've got a meeting with the Bureau brass in a few hours."

Piper glanced sharply at him, surprised. "Why's that? What do they want?"

He shrugged. "To thank us, probably."

Piper was not convinced by this. Still, she could afford to put off her return home a little longer. She would be safe and sound in her cabin soon enough.

"I'll go grab the car," Wade added. "You just sit tight—God knows you could use the rest."

"You're the one with the gimpy leg. I should chauffeur you."

He waved a dismissive hand. "And rob me of the opportunity to prove chivalry ain't dead? Nonsense."

Piper smiled and shook her head, amused by Wade's stubbornness. As she watched him limp off, she became aware of a man standing not far to her right. He looked to be in his forties or early fifties, with a weathered face and a pair of gold-rimmed aviator glasses. He wore a ranger's uniform. He was looking at his phone, but he apparently felt her stare and glanced up.

"Congratulations, by the way," he said with a friendly smile. "You did great work out there."

"Thanks." She shifted her weight from one foot to the other, hoping Wade would return soon. She'd never been very good at small talk.

"Your last name's Woods, right?" the ranger asked.

She nodded. "Why?"

"It's just that I ran into someone by the same name about a year ago. Kind of looked like you, as well, now that I think about it—same eyes."

Piper turned toward him, puzzled. "What are you talking about?"

He shrugged, as if to suggest it was probably of little consequence. "I was at the old ranger station near Havenwood Falls, and this woman showed up asking for directions. I asked her name and she told me it was Ila Woods. It's funny how things come back to you like that."

Piper gasped, unable to believe what she was hearing. "You're sure that was her name? Ila?"

"Yes." Now it was the ranger's turn to look puzzled. "Why?"

All this time, Piper had assumed her mother was dead. But what if she hadn't died? What if she had just disappeared, unable to return home for some reason? The possibility made her heart race with excitement and fear.

"I think that woman was my mother," Piper said, her voice shaky with emotion.

The ranger studied her thoughtfully, waiting for her to speak.

"Did she say where she was going?" Piper asked.

He shrugged again, his expression regretful. "I'm sorry, I can't remember that. I'd completely forgotten about the incident until I heard your name."

Piper's heart sank.

"But I seem to recall she had something in her hand," the ranger continued, as if sensing her disappointment and hoping to ward it off. "She was wearing gloves, and she was holding a flower of some kind—not just a single flower, but a whole column of them together, like a horn. They were bluer even than blueberries, with white at the center. Very striking. I'd tell you what they were, but I've never been much of a botanist." He chuckled sheepishly.

That sounded very much like Ila. She'd always loved wildflowers and would twine them through her hair and Piper's.

Piper, convinced now that the ranger had indeed seen her mother, would have liked to ask a thousand more questions, but she found herself unable to speak, choked by emotion. Wade pulled up, then exited the car and came around to open Piper's door.

The ranger pressed his lips together apologetically. "Sorry if I should've kept that to myself."

"Kept what to himself?" Wade asked Piper in a soft voice.

She swallowed hard and stared into her partner's eyes. "He was talking about my mother. I think…I think she might still be alive."

EPILOGUE

A knot formed in Piper's throat as she stepped into the room, her every movement followed by the stares of half a dozen suited men seated around a polished table.

The room was everything her cabin was not: carpeted, electrically heated, adorned with unremarkable oil paintings and well-kept potted plants. The smell of coffee and ink lingered in the air, filling the space with a sense of urgency. Piper felt out of place in her hiking boots and flannel shirt, but she had no choice but to ignore the discomfort and focus on the task at hand.

"Agent Woods," the director of the FBI said, rising to greet her. "Thank you for coming."

Piper nodded, taking a seat at the table. She could feel the weight of everyone's eyes on her, and she straightened her back, trying to appear composed.

"We wanted to speak with you about your recent work on the Vanessa Johnston case," the director continued. "We've been quite impressed with your skills and resourcefulness."

Piper felt a flicker of pride, but she forced it down. She knew better than to let her guard down around these men, especially before knowing what they wanted.

"Thank you, sir," she said.

"We're also aware of your background in tracking and surveillance," the director went on. "And we believe you could be of great use to us in the future." He paused, letting the words linger in the air.

There it was, the reason for summoning her to this meeting. She should have known.

She shifted in her seat. "I'm sorry. If I'd known what this meeting was about, I'd have told you not to waste your time. I've already made my decision."

The director leaned back, cocking his head at her. "You don't even want to hear what I'm offering?"

"With all due respect, sir, it wouldn't change anything."

The director's eyes flicked to Wade, then back to Piper. He sat forward. "Agent Woods, I think you're making a mistake," he said.

"You have a rare talent for this work, and it would be a shame for it to go to waste."

Piper shook her head. "I appreciate your confidence in me, sir, but I've been doing this for a long time. It's time for me to move on."

"Move on to what?" the director pressed. "You know as well as I do that once you're in this line of work, it's hard to leave. And what else could you do that would be as rewarding as catching criminals and keeping people safe?"

Piper's jaw tightened. She knew he was right, but she couldn't let herself be swayed. "I have my reasons, sir."

"We're prepared to offer you a considerable raise. How would you like to become one of the highest-paid field agents in the Bureau?"

It took a few moments for Piper to absorb what she'd just heard. The offer was very tempting, but she couldn't let money be her only motivation. She had to stay true to herself.

"I'm sorry, sir," she said, her voice firm. "But I can't be bought."

"Skilled and principled," the director said, smiling. "Now I *really* need you to stay on. Lawrence here says you're the best partner he's ever had."

The director turned to Wade, and Piper had the impression he was waiting for Wade to take his side and tell Piper why she should keep working for the Bureau.

Wade let out a long sigh. "Piper's right, sir. It's her decision to make. She's been a valuable asset to the Bureau, but she deserves the freedom to pursue whatever path she chooses."

The director's smile faded, replaced by a look of disappointment. "Very well," he said, rising to his feet. "But know that the offer still stands, Agent Woods. If you ever change your mind, we'll be waiting."

Piper nodded, relieved the meeting was finally over. As the director and his cohorts filed out of the room, Piper turned to Wade, grateful for his support.

"Thank you," she said, smiling at him.

Wade shrugged. "No problem. I just want you to do what's best for you."

Despite his words, she could tell he was disappointed. But was he merely disappointed because she was a good partner, or was there something more personal at play here? She had always felt a spark of attraction between them, but they had never acted on it. Now, as they were left alone in the room, she found herself unable to ignore the tension between them.

"Wade," she said, her voice barely above a whisper. "Can I ask you something?"

"Of course," he said, turning to face her.

"Why did you really support me quitting the Bureau? I mean, I know you said it was because you wanted me to do what was best for me, but was there something else?"

Wade hesitated, his eyes searching hers. "Honestly?" he said finally. "I didn't want to see you get hurt."

Piper furrowed her brow in confusion. "What do you mean? Hurt how?"

Wade sighed, running a hand through his hair. "Pip, you're one of the best agents I've ever worked with. But that doesn't mean you're invincible. I've seen what this job can do to people. I've seen the toll it takes on their lives, their families. And I didn't want to see that happen to you."

Piper said nothing. She was speechless.

"Sometimes," Wade went on, "we have to make hard choices for the sake of our own well-being. And I don't want to see you sacrifice everything for a job that might not be worth it in the end."

Piper felt a wave of emotion wash over her. She had always admired Wade's strength and integrity, but now she saw something else in him—a tenderness, a vulnerability that made her want to reach out and embrace him.

"You're one of the good ones, you know that?" she asked.

He studied her. "You're not upset I dragged you out of your little hermit hole up there in Alaska?"

She laughed softly, then shook her head. "No. I needed this, Wade. With everything that happened before—with how things ended with Fiona—" She trailed off, unsure how to explain the complex emotions she was feeling. Fiona's death had weighed on her every day for the past year, and even though saving Vanessa didn't change what had happened to Fiona, it had given Piper a sense of closure. It had reminded her why she had become an agent in the first place.

"I know," Wade said, his voice soft. "And I'm sorry about Fiona. But I'm glad you're here. I'm glad we're here together."

Piper's heart swelled with an unexpected warmth. She looked into Wade's eyes, seeing something she had never seen before—a vulnerability, a need for connection that mirrored her own.

Piper smiled softly at her partner. "I guess what I'm trying to say is thank you. For everything."

His eyes studied hers solemnly. "It was a pleasure, as always. And if you ever get tired of the woods and want to return to civilization…"

She nodded, understanding. "I know where to find you."

He smiled tiredly at her. "Take care, Pip."

"You too, Wade."

As Piper watched him go, she felt a sense of peace settle over her. The case was over, Vanessa was safe, and the failure of her last case no longer hovered over her the way it had before. She felt free, unburdened by the weight of the past.

It was time to go home.

* * *

A fine snow was drifting down as Piper came within sight of her cabin. It was as she had left it, unharmed, open-armed like the father waiting for the return of his prodigal son.

Piper paused and took a deep breath of the crisp winter air. It was good to be home.

As she entered the cabin, a sense of relief washed over her. The smell of woodsmoke filled her nostrils, and she couldn't help but smile at the familiarity of it all. She had missed this place, missed the peace and quiet it provided. It was a welcome reprieve from the chaos of her life as a Bureau agent.

She kicked off her boots and hung up her coat, built a fire in the stove. As the flames grew, she gathered some herbs together for a cup of tea. She needed something warm after the long journey home.

As she waited for the tea to heat up, she wandered around the cabin, taking in the details she had missed while gone: the rustic wooden walls, the fur rug on the floor, the handmade knickknacks on the shelves. This was her sanctuary, a place where she could escape the world and just be herself.

But there was no escaping the thoughts that came flooding back to her.

Memories of Fiona's death, of Piper's failure to catch her killer, popped into her mind. It was discouraging to know they still haunted her, even after all this time. But she knew she didn't have to run from them anymore. She had faced them head-on, confronting her fears, and she could do so again. She would not be another of Byron Gray's many victims.

As she pulled up a chair by the fire and sipped her tea, she wondered if she had made the right decision by turning the director down. Should she have stayed on with the Bureau and continued to hunt down criminals? Was she wasting her talents by living as a hermit?

She tried to imagine what her parents would have said if they were with her. This led her to thoughts of her mother, and she felt a tremendous sense of yearning, of longing, stir within her.

Was it possible her mother was still alive—had been alive all this time, and Piper hadn't known it?

The thought consumed her, and before she knew it, her mind had drifted off into a deep sleep. She dreamt of her mother, of the times they had spent together, of the love and warmth they had shared before her mother had disappeared without a trace. In her dream, her mother appeared before her, young and vibrant, beckoning her to follow.

Piper followed her mother through a dark forest, the trees twisting and turning into impossible shapes, the ground beneath her feet cold and unforgiving. She called out to her mother, but her voice was swallowed by the darkness.

As she followed her mother, Piper became aware of a presence behind her. She turned, but there was nothing there. A sense of dread settled over her, and she quickened her pace, trying to catch up with her mother.

But as she neared her mother, the forest around them shifted, and Piper found herself standing in a clearing, surrounded by tall trees. Her mother was nowhere to be seen.

Suddenly, she heard a voice behind her. "Hello, Piper."

She spun around, her heart pounding in her chest. Standing before her was Byron Gray, dressed in the tweed outfit he'd worn while using the pseudonym Benjamin Graham.

Piper's mind raced as she tried to process what was happening. She felt a surge of fear, but also anger—how had Gray found her? What did he want?

"Gray," she spat, her hand instinctively moving to her hip where her gun ought to have been. It was not there, however. She was unarmed.

He smiled at her, a sick, twisted grin that made her skin crawl. "Surprised to see me?"

"What do you want?" Piper demanded, trying to keep her voice steady.

Gray took a step toward her. "You, of course. I've been looking for you, Piper. You're the one that got away."

Piper tried to back away, but she was rooted to the spot. She had never felt so helpless.

Gray continued to advance, and Piper knew she was running out of options. She had to fight back, but how could she without a weapon?

As Gray lunged at her, Piper braced herself for impact, but suddenly the ground beneath her feet shifted, and she felt herself falling, falling, falling…

She awoke with a start, her heart pounding in her chest. It had all been a dream, but it had felt terribly real nonetheless.

"It was only a dream," she murmured to herself. "Only a dream."

Despite this reassurance, she had no desire to go back to sleep. Instead she threw the blankets back, crawled out of bed, and got dressed.

Plucking her rifle off the wall, she opened the door and stepped outside. It was dark, and the air was heavy and still, the forest bathed with moonlight.

Searching the wilderness with her gaze, Piper thought of all the times she'd gone to her mother as a child, asking for an interpretation of a dream she'd had. Her mother had always been a reassuring presence, a source of comfort and wisdom.

Closing her eyes, Piper summoned up a picture of her mother's face. She thought of the flowers the ranger had mentioned, deep blue with white at the center. A whole column of them, he'd said, "like a horn."

As Piper thought about it, she began to wonder what type of flower her mother had been carrying. Not many plants in nature were "bluer even than blueberries." So what could it have been?

Recalling all the flowers she knew of that matched the description the ranger had given her, she realized he must have been talking about delphinium. It was a beautiful flower, tall and majestic, notoriously difficult to grow.

And it also happened to be very toxic. Deadly, even.

Piper's eyes sprang open, and her heart leapt as her mind turned over a new theory.

Ila Woods knew better than to handle a plant as poisonous as delphinium if she didn't have to, and she wasn't the kind of person to pick a plant just because it looked pretty. Piper could think of only one realistic reason why Ila would have been carrying such a plant around.

Mom was sending me a message, she thought. *And not just any message, but a warning. But what kind of warning? What does it mean?*

There was only one way to find out: She would have to track her mother down.

And she would have to do so on her own.

NOW AVAILABLE!

SOMEWHERE SANE
(A Piper Woods FBI Suspense Thriller—Book Two)

Former FBI Special Agent Piper Woods, expert tracker and survivalist, left the force behind after a traumatizing case to live far off the grid. Determined not to go back, she is nonetheless needed when an elusive, nomadic killer strikes in the Southwestern desert, in an area so remote and harsh that only someone like Piper could survive. In a deadly cat and mouse thriller, Piper must hunt her prey and save the next victim before it's too late—all while being hunted by the demons of her past....

"Molly Black has written a taut thriller that will keep you on the edge of your seat… I absolutely loved this book and can't wait to read the next book in the series!"
—Reader review for Girl One: Murder

SOMEWHERE SANE is book #2 in a long anticipated new series by critically-acclaimed and #1 bestselling mystery and suspense author Molly Black, whose books have received over 2,000 five-star reviews and ratings.

A page-turning and harrowing crime thriller featuring a brilliant and tortured FBI agent, the Piper Woods series is a riveting mystery, packed with non-stop action, suspense, twists and turns, revelations, and driven by a breakneck pace that will keep you flipping pages late into the night. Fans of Rachel Caine, Teresa Driscoll and Robert Dugoni are sure to fall in love.

Future books in the series are also available.

"I binge read this book. It hooked me in and didn't stop till the last few pages… I look forward to reading more!"
—Reader review for Found You

"I loved this book! Fast-paced plot, great characters and interesting insights into investigating cold cases. I can't wait to read the next book!"
—Reader review for Girl One: Murder

"Very good book… You will feel like you are right there looking for the kidnapper! I know I will be reading more in this series!"
—Reader review for Girl One: Murder

"This is a very well written book and holds your interest from page 1… Definitely looking forward to reading the next one in the series, and hopefully others as well!"
—Reader review for Girl One: Murder

"Wow, I cannot wait for the next in this series. Starts with a bang and just keeps going."
—Reader review for Girl One: Murder

"Well written book with a great plot, one that will keep you up at night. A page turner!"
—Reader review for Girl One: Murder

"A great suspense that keeps you reading… can't wait for the next in this series!"
—Reader review for Found You

"Sooo soo good! There are a few unforeseen twists… I binge read this like I binge watch Netflix. It just sucks you in."
—Reader review for Found You

Molly Black

Bestselling author Molly Black is author of the MAYA GRAY FBI suspense thriller series, comprising nine books (and counting); of the RYLIE WOLF FBI suspense thriller series, comprising six books; of the TAYLOR SAGE FBI suspense thriller series, comprising eight books; of the KATIE WINTER FBI suspense thriller series, comprising eleven books (and counting); of the RUBY HUNTER FBI suspense thriller series, comprising five books (and counting); of the CAITLIN DARE FBI suspense thriller series, comprising six books (and counting); of the REESE LINK mystery series, comprising six books (and counting); of the CLAIRE KING FBI suspense thriller series, comprising five books (and counting); and of the PIPER WOODS mystery series, comprising five books (and counting).

An avid reader and lifelong fan of the mystery and thriller genres, Molly loves to hear from you, so please feel free to visit www.mollyblackauthor.com to learn more and stay in touch.

BOOKS BY MOLLY BLACK

PIPER WOODS FBI SUSPENSE THRILLER
SOMEWHERE SAFE (Book #1)
SOMEWHERE SANE (Book #2)
SOMEWHERE WHOLE (Book #3)
SOMEWHERE FAR (Book #4)
SOMEWHERE WRONG (Book #5)

CAITLIN DARE FBI SUSPENSE THRILLER
COME GET ME (Book #1)
COME FIND ME (Book #2)
COME TAKE ME (Book #3)
COME CATCH ME (Book #4)
COME SAVE ME (Book #5)
COME STOP ME (Book #6)

MAYA GRAY MYSTERY SERIES
GIRL ONE: MURDER (Book #1)
GIRL TWO: TAKEN (Book #2)
GIRL THREE: TRAPPED (Book #3)
GIRL FOUR: LURED (Book #4)
GIRL FIVE: BOUND (Book #5)
GIRL SIX: FORSAKEN (Book #6)
GIRL SEVEN: CRAVED (Book #7)
GIRL EIGHT: HUNTED (Book #8)
GIRL NINE: GONE (Book #9)

RYLIE WOLF FBI SUSPENSE THRILLER
FOUND YOU (Book #1)
CAUGHT YOU (Book #2)
SEE YOU (Book #3)
WANT YOU (Book #4)
TAKE YOU (Book #5)
DARE YOU (Book #6)

TAYLOR SAGE FBI SUSPENSE THRILLER

DON'T LOOK (Book #1)
DON'T BREATHE (Book #2)
DON'T RUN (Book #3)
DON'T FLINCH (Book #4)
DON'T REMEMBER (Book #5)
DON'T TELL (Book #6)

KATIE WINTER FBI SUSPENSE THRILLER

SAVE ME (Book #1)
REACH ME (Book #2)
HIDE ME (Book #3)
BELIEVE ME (Book #4)
HELP ME (Book #5)
FORGET ME (Book #6)
HOLD ME (Book #7)
PROTECT ME (Book #8)
REMEMBER ME (Book #9)
CATCH ME (Book #10)
WATCH ME (Book #11)

RUBY HUNTER FBI SUSPENSE THRILLER

IF I RUN (Book #1)
IF I TELL (Book #2)
IF I LIVE (Book #3)
IF I FORGET (Book #4)
IF I RETURN (Book #5)

CAITLIN DARE FBI SUSPENSE THRILLER

COME GET ME (Book #1)
COME FIND ME (Book #2)
COME TAKE ME (Book #3)
COME CATCH ME (Book #4)
COME SAVE ME (Book #5)

REESE LINK MYSTERY

BEYOND REASON (Book #1)
BEYOND REACH (Book #2)
BEYOND REPAIR (Book #3)

BEYOND DOUBT (Book #4)
BEYOND NORMAL (Book #5)
BEYOND HOPE (Book #6)

Made in the USA
Monee, IL
26 May 2024